A movement, out of the corner of my eye, caused the hairs on my arms to prickle. I'd known better than to stay in this empty room. But I was here now and running would make it worse. I turned to face the same soul from outside sitting in a chair at the back of the classroom with his feet propped up on the desk in front of him and his arms crossed casually over his chest. How had he known I could see him? I'd given no indication outside. Normally ghosts needed a little clue from me to realize I wasn't as blind as the rest of the world. Something was different with this one. I dropped my gaze and started to turn around. Maybe I should go join Miranda and the jock squad out in the hall. If I acted like I didn't see him and casually made my way back into the hallway then he might think he'd made a mistake and float away or walk through a wall or something.

"You don't really want to subject yourself to such pointless company, do you?" A cold, smooth voice broke the silence.

I gripped the hard plastic chair beside me so hard that my knuckles turned white. I fought down a startled little cry—almost a scream—in the back of my throat. Should I ignore him? Should I respond? Alerting him that his hunch was right might not end well. But ignoring this was going to be impossible. He could speak. Souls never talked to me. From the time I realized that the strangers who frequently watched me or appeared in my home and wandered the halls were not visible to anyone but me, I'd started ignoring them. Seeing dead people wasn't a new thing for me but having them talk to me was definitely a new twist.

"I pegged you with more guts. Are you going to let me down too?" His tone softened. There was a familiar drawl in his voice now.

"You can speak," I said looking directly at him, I needed him to know I wasn't afraid. I'd been dealing with wandering souls, which is what I like to think of them as, all my life. They didn't frighten me but I liked to ignore them so they would go away. If they ever thought I could see them, they followed me. He continued to watch me with an amused expression on his face. I noticed his crooked grin produced a single dimple. The dimple didn't seem to fit with his cold, arrogant demeanor. As much as his presence annoyed me, I couldn't help but admit this soul could only be labeled as ridiculously gorgeous.

"Yes, I speak. Were you expecting me to be mute?"

I leaned my hip against the desk. "Yes, as a matter of fact, I was. You're the first one who has ever spoken to me."

# Existence
## by
## Abbi Glines

**Wild Child Publishing.com**
*Culver City, California*

Editor: Brandy Cowan

ISBN: 978-1-61798-014-5 – ebook
978-1-61798-021-3 – print

If you are interested in purchasing more works of this nature, please stop by www.wildchildpublishing.com.

Wild Child Publishing.com
P.O. Box 4897
Culver City, CA 90231-4897

Printed in The United States of America

# Dedication

*To my husband, Keith. Without his support I wouldn't have been able to finish the first book. His understanding and patience mean the world to me. I love you honey.*

# Acknowledgments

*I have to start by thanking my kids, who tolerated the dirty house, lack of clean clothes, and my mood swings, while I wrote this book. They are my world.*

*My best friend, Monica, who once again read it from start to finish in less than twenty- four hours in all it's rough draft glory to give me her opinion.*

*My mom, Becky, who tells anyone who will stand still long enough about my books and where they can find them. Her unconditional support means the world to me.*

*My dad, Joe, who passed on the ability to spin a story to me. He doesn't get acknowledged for this often enough but I am incredibly thankful for this gift.*

*The Paranormal Plumes: www.theplumessociety.com*

*Without this bunch of amazing authors I don't know where I'd be. They aren't just authors whose stories I adore but they've become friends I truly love. The advice, encouragement, last minute editing, and all other forms of support I get from this group is priceless.*

# Chapter One

*Don't look at him and he'll go away.* I chanted in my head, as I walked toward my locker. It took an extreme amount of willpower not to glance back over my shoulder. Not only would alerting him I could see him be pointless but it would also be stupid. The halls were already full of students. Although, if he'd followed me inside the school I would have seen him easily enough through the throngs of people. He would stand out just like they always did, unmoving and watching.

"GAH! Have you seen Leif? I mean honestly can he get any hotter? Oh, yes he can." Miranda Wouters, my best friend since elementary school, squealed as she grabbed my arm.

"No, I haven't seen him. Football camp must've agreed with him," I replied, forcing a smile. I couldn't care less how hot Leif Montgomery looked. Miranda rolled her eyes and opened the locker beside mine.

"Honestly, Pagan, I don't get how you can be so immune to such intense hotness."

I managed a genuine laugh and slipped my bag over my shoulder. "Hotness? You didn't just say hotness."

Miranda shrugged, "I'm not an endless well of descriptive words, like you are."

I chanced a peek over my shoulder. The halls were full of normal people, living people. They were talking, laughing, and reading over their schedules. It was all very real. I let out a sigh of relief. This was the first day of my senior year. I wanted to enjoy it.

"So, what class do you have first?" I asked, relaxing for the first time since I'd spotted the dead guy lounging outside on the picnic table staring directly at me.

"I have Algebra II, blah! I so enjoyed Geometry last year. I hated Algebra my freshman year and I can already feel the negative vibes coming from my textbook." Miranda's dramatic flair for life never failed to make me smile.

"I've got English Lit."

"Well, we all know you're loving that. OH, look, look, look, there he is," Miranda managed to squeal in a hushed tone while nodding her head toward where Leif stood talking to other football players.

"Hate that I can't hang around and bask in the presence of greatness with you, but this is my stop." Miranda glanced back at me, rolled her big brown eyes, and gave me a wave before making her way over to Leif.

Empty rooms were places I usually avoided at all cost. Given the fact the bell wouldn't ring for five more minutes, this room would no doubt remain empty for the next four minutes. If I'd stayed out in the hall, I would have been dragged by Miranda over to where Leif stood surrounded by his chosen few. I knew without a doubt he wasn't interested in talking to Miranda. We'd been going to school with Leif since we were eleven. Since his move from somewhere up north to the coastal town of Breeze, Florida, never had he acknowledged either of us. Not that I minded. He wasn't my type. I walked over to the desk closest to the window and put my bag down.

A movement, out of the corner of my eye, caused the hairs on my arms to prickle. I'd known better than to stay in this empty room. But I was here now and running would make it worse. I turned to face the same soul from outside sitting in a chair at the back of the classroom with his feet propped up on the desk in front of him and his arms crossed casually over his chest. How had he known I could see him? I'd given no indication outside. Normally ghosts needed a little clue from me to realize I wasn't as blind as the rest of the world. Something was different with this one. I dropped my gaze and started to turn around. Maybe I should go join Miranda and the jock squad out in the hall. If I acted like I didn't see him and casually made my way back into the hallway then he might think he'd made a mistake and float away or walk through a wall or something.

"You don't really want to subject yourself to such pointless company, do you?" A cold, smooth voice broke the silence.

I gripped the hard plastic chair beside me so hard that my knuckles turned white. I fought down a startled little cry—almost a scream—in the back of my throat. Should I ignore him? Should I respond? Alerting him that his hunch was right might not end well. But ignoring this was going to be impossible. He could speak. Souls never talked to me. From the time I realized that the strangers who frequently watched me or appeared in my home and wandered the halls were not visible to anyone but me, I'd started ignoring them. Seeing dead people wasn't a new thing for me but having them talk to me was definitely a new twist.

"I pegged you with more guts. Are you going to let me down

too?" His tone softened. There was a familiar drawl in his voice now.

"You can speak," I said looking directly at him, I needed him to know I wasn't afraid. I'd been dealing with wandering souls, which is what I like to think of them as, all my life. They didn't frighten me but I liked to ignore them so they would go away. If they ever thought I could see them, they followed me. He continued to watch me with an amused expression on his face. I noticed his crooked grin produced a single dimple. The dimple didn't seem to fit with his cold, arrogant demeanor. As much as his presence annoyed me, I couldn't help but admit this soul could only be labeled as ridiculously gorgeous.

"Yes, I speak. Were you expecting me to be mute?"

I leaned my hip against the desk. "Yes, as a matter of fact, I was. You're the first one who has ever spoken to me."

A frown creased his forehead. "The first one?"

He appeared genuinely surprised he wasn't the first dead person I could see. He was definitely the most unique soul I'd ever seen. Ignoring a soul who could talk was going to be hard. However, I needed to get over his ability and get rid of him. Talking to invisible friends could hinder my social life. I'd end up looking like some crazy chick who talked to herself.

"Pagan Moore, this must be my lucky day." At the sound of my name, I spun around to see Wyatt Tucker sauntering into the room.

I forced a smile as if I hadn't been speaking to an empty room. "I guess it is." I tilted my head back to meet his eyes. "You just keep growing, don't you?"

"Can't seem to stop it." He winked and then slung a long leg over the chair across from mine before sitting down. "What have you been up to this summer? I haven't seen much of you."

I chanced a peek back toward the soul to find an empty chair. A mixture of relief and disappointment washed over me. Wanting to ask him more questions wasn't exactly a good idea, but I couldn't help it. I›d asked other souls questions before like, «Why are you following me?» or, «Why can I see you?» and they always remained mute. Often times they disappeared when I began asking them questions.

Turning my attention back to Wyatt, I forced a smile before replying, "I stayed up in North Carolina all summer at my Aunt's horse ranch."

Wyatt leaned back in his chair and shook his head. "I just don't get why people would want to leave all summer when we live on one of the most beautiful beaches in the world."

For me it hadn't been a choice really but I didn't want to explain the reason to Wyatt or anyone else. More students started entering the room, followed by our English Literature teacher, Mr. Brown.

"Wyatt, what's up, Slim," Justin Gregory called out as he made his way toward us. He plopped his bag onto the desk across from Wyatt. For now, Wyatt's attention was off me thanks to Justin's interruption. As I turned toward the front of the class, my eyes once again found the soul. Leaning against the wall directly diagonal to my desk, he stood watching me. I glared at him and he seemed to find my obvious dislike entertaining. His dimple appeared and I hated the fact I found it sexy. This wasn't a human, well not anymore. It took extreme willpower to turn my gaze away from him and focus my attention on the board where Mr. Brown had written our assignment. I'd always ignored these pesky souls before and they'd gone away. I'd just have to get over the fact this one could talk to me. If I didn't ignore him I'd be stuck with him stalking me.

"Hate it, I mean, like hate it in a big way," Miranda grumbled as she dropped her lunch tray down on the table with a loud clank. "If I have to sit through Algebra and Chemistry all morning, you'd think that I at least could've a little eye candy in one of my classes. But noooooo! I get Gretchen with her relentless sniffles and Craig with his gas issues."

I choked on my sandwich and grabbed my bottle of water to take a quick gulp in order to wash down my food. Once I felt sure I wasn't going to choke to death, I glanced up at Miranda's concerned face. "Do you have to say things like that when I've got a mouth full of food?" I asked.

She shrugged. "Sorry, I'm just sayin' is all. I didn't mean for you to forget to chew your food." She reached over and squeezed my arm. "There goes his perfectness now. Do you think he's going to hook back up with Kendra this year? I mean they really had a bad breakup last year with all the cheating and stuff. Surely he's going to move on."

I took another bite of my sandwich, not wanting to answer her question. I didn't care who Leif Montgomery hooked up with but, yes, I felt most certain he would hook back up with Kendra. They happen to be the 'golden couple'. Everyone knew this and expected it. Their type always lived up to their name.

"Pull your tongue back in your mouth, Miranda. You look like a dog in need of water." Wyatt sat down across from us, chuckling at his own joke while Miranda scowled at him.

"I don't have my tongue hanging out, thank you very much."

Wyatt winked at me and shrugged. "Looked like it to me. What do you think, Pagan, was she drooling or what?"

I crammed another bite into my mouth. I wasn't getting in the middle of this one. Wyatt started laughing as I pointed to my over-stuffed mouth. Miranda elbowed me in the side. "Don't go taking his side. He's just mean."

With a large gulp of water I washed down my food, and then stared pointedly at Miranda. "You two can hash this out all you want but I'm not getting into this. Ever since you decided to take friendship a step further last year and it came crashing down around you, all ya'll want to do is take cheap shots at each other. Not my fight. Leave me alone." I quickly took another bite so I wouldn't be asked to say anything else. When the two of them realized that they drove each other nuts because they hadn't gotten over one another, it would make my life easier. Then again, I'd be the one alone. My boyfriend, Jay Potts, had moved away months ago and I hadn't spoken to him since before I'd left for my Aunt's this summer.

"That's not what this is about! I could care less that he couldn't keep his tongue out of Katie's throat when I wasn't looking," Miranda said angrily.

"I didn't have my tongue down anyone's throat but yours, Miranda, but you don't believe me and I'm tired of defending myself." Wyatt stood and yanked his tray of untouched food up before stalking away.

"Asshole," she murmured, watching him relocate to the jock table.

I hated seeing them like this. The three of us had been friends since third grade. Back then, Wyatt had been all arms and legs. Now, he towered over everyone with his long, muscular body. Miranda hadn't been immune to his sudden stud qualities last year. Now, she couldn't stand him.

"Listen, Miranda, I was thinking, maybe if you two talked about what happened without you accusing him, things might work out." I'd tried this before and she always ignored me.

11

Sure enough, she started shaking her head causing her brown curls to bounce back and forth. "I know what happened, Pagan. I don't want to talk it out with him. He's a big, cheating liar." She took a violent chomp out of her Granny Smith apple and continued glaring in Wyatt's direction. "Look at him acting like he fits in over at that table. I mean, really, who does he think he is?"

I followed her gaze. Wyatt sat leaning back in a chair, laughing at something another basketball player was saying. They all seemed pleased to have Wyatt in their presence. Normally he sat with us. This year things would be different. I sighed, wishing I didn't have to be the one to point out the obvious to Miranda. "He is the only guy in this school who has college scouts coming to his basketball games to watch him play. That's who he is. Leif may be the big Kahuna on the football field, but I don't see any college scouts knocking on his door. You can be mad at Wyatt, but he belongs at that table more than anyone else."

Miranda turned her glare on me and instantly it transformed into a frown. "Well, he can go to college on a basketball scholarship and cheat on all those cheerleaders, then. I should warn them all." Her voice had taken on a defeated tone as she stood up and walked toward the garbage cans. I watched her, wishing I could find a way to fix this thing between the two of them.

Someone sat down beside me in the chair Miranda had just vacated. I turned in my seat, half expecting to see the soul. Imagine my surprise when it wasn't the unwanted soul but the arrogant jock.

# Chapter Two

"Hey, Pagan, Mr. Yorkley said I needed to come talk to you." Leif's voice seemed to snap me out of my momentary shock. If Mr. Yorkley sent him, he needed some sort of academic help. However, I wasn't sure I wanted to help, nor did I intend on making this easy for him. I managed a "so what" expression and waited in silence. Leif cleared his throat and rubbed his hands on the knees of his jeans, as if he were actually nervous.

"Uh, um, well," he began, "I mean, that is, I need some help in Speech. It isn't my thing and Mr. Yorkley said you were the one to talk to about getting some assistance." He stared straight ahead as he spoke. He hadn't even glanced over at me. I really didn't like this guy. He finally turned his gaze my direction. I was sure he bestowed this pitifully hopeful expression on females everywhere, in order to get what he wanted. My stomach betrayed me and quivered from the affect his pleading baby blue eyes evoked. I hated that he could make my body react to him at all, other than to hurl of course.

"This is the first day of school. How can you need help already?" I asked in a voice I hoped sounded annoyed. I wasn't a simpering idiot who could be moved by a few bats of his long eyelashes, even if my double-crossing body didn't seem to agree. Surely I was imagining the faint blush on his cheeks.

"Um, yeah, I know, but I, well, that is Mr. Yorkley and I know I'm going to struggle," he said a little defensively. Leif had always been a good student. I'd been in a few classes with him.

"Why do you both think you'll struggle? Surely, you're not afraid to speak out loud in class."

He shook his head and stared straight ahead again. "No, that's not it." I waited but he didn't say anymore. Interestingly enough, I became intrigued.

"I don't really know why you need my help. It's really simple. You write speeches about the topics assigned and then give them orally. Simple, basic, no fancy strings or hard equations."

He turned his gaze back toward me with a sad smile. "It isn't so easy for me." He paused and acted like he wanted to say more, and then he shook his head and stood up, "Never mind, forget I asked." I watched him walk past the table of his admiring fans and head outside through the double doors. I experienced a minute pang of guilt for being so hard on him. He'd come to ask for help and I'd basically just made fun of him. I reached for my tray, angry with myself for acting like a jerk. 'Jerk' belonged in *his* job description, not mine.

My book bag landed on the kitchen counter with a heavy thump, announcing my return. I headed for the fridge. The fresh squeezed orange juice I'd worked so hard on yesterday sounded good.

"Pagan, honey, is that you?" my mom's voice called from down the hall. She was huddled in the corner of her office with a large cup of coffee, typing away on her computer. I didn't have to see her to know this. My mother is a writer. She lives in stained sweats behind her computer.

"Yes," I replied. Before I could pour myself a glass of orange juice, the sound of her slippers flopping against the hardwood floors surprised me. This was a strange occurrence. Rarely did she break away from her writing when I came home from school. It was usually closer to dinner time before she graced me with her presence.

"Good, I'm glad you came straight home. I need to talk to you and then I have to get dressed." She motioned to her baggy sweats and large Atlanta Braves t-shirt. "I'm having dinner with Roger but don't worry, I'm leaving you money to order a pizza." She pulled a bar stool out and her friendly face turned serious. It wasn't a good serious, either. This was the kind of serious I recognized but rarely experienced.

"What?" I asked as I set my glass down.

Mom's back became more rigid as she cleared her throat. The "I am disappointed in you" frown turned the corners of her lips down. I quickly racked my brain, trying to think of something I might have done to upset her, but nothing came to mind.

"I received a call, right in the middle of chapter fifteen, from Mr. Yorkley."

Uh oh, she knew about Leif. "Mr. Yorkley?" I asked, pretending I didn't know what this was about. Mom nodded and tilted her head to the side as if she were studying me to see if she believed I really had no idea why my teacher might call. The head tilt always made me nervous. I braced myself. She was about to let me have it. I'd been a jerk, but in my defense it wasn't like I did any damage. I'd made fun of the reigning king, not someone with low self-esteem.

"Apparently, there is a young man who has a learning disability and was told to seek you out for extra tutoring. You did sign up to tutor this year for extra credit. My question is: why, Pagan, would you not help a student at your school who struggles with something as serious as dyslexia? The boy, I'm told, has the opportunity to be given a scholarship on his athletic abilities, but his handicap requires he get extra help in certain classes. He needs someone to help him put the speeches he must write on paper. That doesn't seem like too much to ask. You did say you wanted to tutor this year. Explain to me why you chose to tell this boy no, and I'm telling you now it had better be good." She leaned back and crossed her arms over her chest, in her "I'm waiting" stance.

Leif suffered from dyslexia? Was this a joke? I'd been going to school with him most of my life. Girls, Miranda included, knew everything about him. Heck, Miranda once told me exactly where his birthmark happened to be located. Not that I cared. How could Leif Montgomery have dyslexia and no one know it?

I thought back to Leif asking me for help in the lunchroom today and the way I'd acted. The revelation that Leif dealt with something like dyslexia and still managed to make such good grades bothered me. I wasn't sure why, exactly, but it did. I liked thinking of him as a jock. Someone who managed to get heaps of good fortune dumped on his head. Now all I could think about was the way he looked today when he'd come to ask me for help. A sick knot settled in the pit of my stomach.

I glanced up at my mom and shook my head slowly, "I had no idea he had a learning disability. He's always so cocky and sure of himself. I was surprised he came to me for help and I immediately questioned why he, of all people, would need help."

Mom leaned forward on the bar and her frown eased some. "Well, you can make it right. I've raised a more compassionate child than that."

I nodded and reached for my book bag, "I know and I'm sorry. I'll fix it."

She seemed appeased. "I don't like getting calls from school about you. Especially not when I'm writing an intense murder scene."

I smiled and put my glass into the dishwasher before turning back to her. "Sorry, I'll try to remember that. Um, so, second date then with this Roger guy?"

She blushed. "Yes, he and I seem to be able to talk for hours.

I love his mind and he has traveled all over the world. My mind is always turning when he talks of places and things I've never seen."

She shrugged, "You know me, I'm always thinking of a story behind everything."

I raised my eyebrows and leaned close to her. "And he's a hottie."

She giggled, which was not a normal sound for my mom to make. "Oh, now that's not why I like him. It's his mind and the conversation."    ·

I laughed out loud. "Sure it is, Mom, you just keep telling yourself that lie."

"Okay fine, he's rather attractive."

"Mom, he's a hottie and you know it. Granted, he's an old hottie, but still."

"He's not old. He's my age."

"Exactly."

I watched her attempt to appear hurt before she gave in and laughed. "Fine, I'm old. Your money will be on the counter when you're ready to order some pizza."

Staying home by myself wasn't something I enjoyed. When I'm alone the souls I see wandering aimlessly bother me. Especially since I'd actually chatted with one today. It was easier to remind myself they were harmless when they were mute. Now, I was a little freaked out. Once I closed my bedroom door, I grabbed the cell out of my pocket and called Miranda.


"Let me see if I've got this straight." Miranda sat on the couch with a piece of pizza in her hand and a soda between her legs, staring at me. "Leif 'rocking-hot-make-you-melt' Montgomery asked you to help him in Speech and you turned him down? Are you as insane as I think you are? I mean really, Pagan, I thought the insaneness you so often flash about was just for show and deep down you did have some common sense."

I slapped a piece of pizza down on the plate in front of me in frustration. "I'm going to fix it in the morning. It isn't like I robbed a bank. Stop making a big deal out of it. I know I screwed up. He really needed help and I did sign up to tutor. If I want the extra credit, I have to help those Mr. Yorkley sends my way."

Miranda rolled her eyes, "Oh, and heaven forbid he send the

hottest male in the county your way! I mean, for crying out loud, what is wrong with you?"

It was impossible not to find amusement in her drama. Miranda never failed to make you smile at the little things, by making it all a big dramatic scene.

"I was wrong for not offering to help. I guess my prejudice toward jocks got in the way. But, I'm not helping him because you think he is hot. I'm only helping because he actually needs help and I signed up to help those who need it."

Miranda rolled her eyes and froze, holding her pizza in mid-air between the plate and her mouth. "Wait....is he like going to come to your house and stuff? Because, if he is, I want to be here too. He can notice me and realize he's hopelessly in love with me and then we can date through high school and then after graduation, we can get married and I can have his babies."

Soda spewed from my mouth and coated my plate of pizza. "What?" She smiled and shrugged before taking a bite of her soda-free pizza.

"For starters, you need to finish college before you can even think of getting married and having kids. And NO he won't be coming over here. Even if he was, I wouldn't let you come over after such an insane comment. The last thing I want to do is fix my friend up with a guy she's fantasizing about marrying and having babies with straight out of high school."

Miranda sighed in defeat and gave me the pouty frown she was so good at. "You're no fun, Pagan, no fun at all."

I took another piece of pizza from the cardboard box I'd placed on the coffee table. "Really? So, why do you keep me around?" I asked.

"Because I love you!"

"Love you too."

Miranda stood up. "I hate to leave all the warm coziness of this conversation but I need to go pee." She jumped up off the couch and headed down the hall toward the bathroom. She always held it to the last minute. I kept thinking she would grow out of it as we got older but she hadn't. When she decided she needed to go to the restroom it was always a mad rush.

"Interesting friend you have there. She's really quite entertaining." The pizza I'd been lifting toward my mouth fell out of my hands and into my lap. I bit back the scream in my throat. He'd startled me but I recognized the deep drawl.

The talking soul sat on one of my bar stools. Just great. The really sexy, yet creepy-because—he-can-talk dead guy must have followed me home. "Why're you here?" I demanded quietly, wanting him to just leave me alone and go wander the Earth somewhere else. The intensity of his steady gaze made my pulse jump from nerves, or maybe a better description would be fear.

"I can't tell you that. Now isn't the time. But, I can tell you I'm not going away anytime soon."

After a quick peek to see if Miranda was returning, I glanced back at him. "Why? If I ignore you—you soul things—you always go away."

He frowned, leaned forward and studied me closely. "What do you mean by ignore you 'soul things'?"

Not feeling very safe on the floor looking up at him, I shoved the pizza out of my lap and stood up so I could be eye level with the soul. "You aren't special. I've been seeing ghosts or souls or spirits or whatever you are, all my life. Souls are everywhere. In my house, on the street, in the stores, at others' houses, I can see them. I just ignore them and they go away."

He slowly stood up and took a step toward me. His height was intimidating but his nearness would have had me backing up even if he'd been short. "You can see souls?"

"I can see you, can't I?"

He nodded slowly. "Yes, but I'm different. You're supposed to see me. It's easier that way. But the others....you aren't supposed to see them."

The bathroom door opened with a click. I jerked my head around to see Miranda returning with a smile on her face. "Were you talking to yourself just now?"

I shrugged and forced a smile. "Um, yes."

She laughed and sat back down on the couch. I took a steadying breath and then glanced back at the soul who had returned to the same white wicker kitchen stool, watching me. The only way I could finish this conversation and get him to leave would be to send Miranda home. Talking to a soul she couldn't see wouldn't go over very well. My ability to see souls wasn't something I'd shared with her and I didn't intend to start.

The soul seemed to be waiting for me to make a decision. The thought of being alone with him frightened me. He might be sexy, but he was dead and he had followed me home. Creepy didn't begin to describe it. Letting Miranda leave me here wouldn't be in the plans tonight. I put some distance between the soul and myself by walking over to the couch to sit next to Miranda. "Want to watch Vampire Diaries? I have the last two episodes recorded," I asked her, hoping the soul got the hint and vanished.

"OH! Yes, I missed last week."

I grabbed the remote, scanned down the recorded shows on my DVR list and clicked play. I needed to get my mind off the dead guy in the room. After at least ten minutes of listening to Miranda swoon over Damon and fuss at Elena, I held my breath and chanced a peek in his direction. The stool where he'd been sitting now sat empty. I let out a sigh of relief.


All morning, I'd been replaying exactly what I would to say to Leif. I wasn't sure if I should let him know that I knew about his dyslexia, or if I should just tell him we could start as soon as he was ready and skip the explanation. I also prepared myself for him to tell me he no longer needed my help. If he'd already managed to find another tutor then this whole mess would be over. I wouldn't be forced to help someone I didn't really like, but it would be a nega-tive strike against my extra credit. Either way, I lost in this situa-tion. This also wasn't something I wanted to do with Miranda be-side me, batting her eyelashes at him and giggling when he spoke. Timing would be of utmost importance. After Chemistry, I waited in the hallway for him to come out of the only class we shared this semester. Luckily, he walked out alone.

"Um, Leif, could I talk to you a minute?" I asked as soon as he stepped out of the door. He glanced over at me and an immediate frown creased his forehead. He appeared to be seriously consider-ing walking away and ignoring me when he turned and made his way over to stand in front of me instead. Leaning against the wall, he crossed his arms in front of his chest and waited. I had a feeling he wasn't going to make this easy for me.

"About yesterday, I'm sorry I was so rude about helping you. I did sign up to tutor for extra credit and I shouldn't have treated you the way I did." I stopped and hesitated, hoping he would say some-thing. He didn't move or even act as if he was going to respond. I took a deep breath and reminded myself this was my fault. "If you still want me to tutor you, I'd be happy to," I finished, not really happy, but it sounded like the polite thing to say and his silent stare happened to be making me nervous. He appeared bored and it took extreme self-control not to get mad at him and walk off. Remembering exactly how rude I'd been yesterday helped keep me waiting patiently for his reply. He straightened and stared down the hall over my shoulder as if he wasn't really considering what I'd said.

Right when I felt positive he no longer wanted my help, he focused his bored expression on me and asked, "Are you offering because of Mr. Yorkley? Did he make you do this?"

I thought of my Mom's words yesterday and wondered. If she hadn't insisted I 'make it right', would I be offering my help now? This popular, talented, worshipped guy trusted me with his secret. I didn't like him. Heck, I didn't know him, but for some reason I wanted to help him.

"I acted the way I did because I just don't like you very much. I was wrong and, honestly, I don't even know you well enough to form an opinion of you. I'm offering to help because you need it. That's what I signed up for and that's why I'm here now."

He seemed to think about what I said for a moment, and then a small smile appeared on his face. "You don't like me, huh?"

I stood a little straighter and pulled my books closer to my chest feeling defensive. Surprisingly, it was rather difficult to be the recipient of one of his charming smiles. Especially after I'd just admitted I didn't like him. Why did he have to be so frustratingly cute? I gave a small shake of my head and he chuckled. "Well, we might have to work on changing your mind." He slipped his book bag up higher on his shoulder and flashed me one more grin. "I'll see you later."

He walked away, leaving me slightly flustered. I fought the urge to turn around and watch him saunter off. A slow, clapping noise startled me and I spun around to see the talking soul leaning against the lockers with that blasted, crooked grin.

"Impressive. A female with enough nerve to admit she can be wrong, apologize, and offer to rectify the situation."

I rolled my eyes and sighed, knowing the hallway wasn't completely empty so responding wouldn't be possible. "Go away," I hissed anyway, before turning to head for the cafeteria.

# Chapter Three

I stood in my living room, frustrated over losing control of the situation in my meeting with Leif. I'd gone to the library prepared to set up our scheduled tutoring and I'd even made notes in the handbook Mr. Yorkley gave to all the tutors. I'd gone to the trouble of creating a schedule for Leif to use, making notes of the days and times of our sessions. I wrote out instructions for him on what to bring and how to take notes in class. Everything seemed so cut and dry. Yet, nothing had gone as planned. I hadn't taken into consideration that studying with Leif last period would be impossible since all football players must report to the field during last period. I also hadn't thought about his afternoon practices and his evening job at his uncle's surf shop. The doorbell rang before I could get any more upset over nothing going the way I'd planned. I couldn't shake my irritation as I opened the door.

Leif smiled apologetically, "I'm really sorry about this. I feel bad you're having to work around my schedule. I know seven is late and, well, I'm sorry."

The steam I'd managed to work up all evening as I'd thought about having to work around Leif evaporated. He seemed sincere and a little nervous. This wasn't the way I expected him to act. Where was his arrogance? Was he always so nice? Surely not. The guy had dated the wicked witch of the southern coast for two years. I stepped back to let him in.

"That's okay. Go ahead and sit at the table and I'll get us something to drink. Do you like root beer?" I asked, walking toward the fridge so I wouldn't have to look at him.

"That's great, thanks."

I took my time, getting the sodas out of the fridge and opening them before walking back to the kitchen table. This would be the first time I'd ever really talked to Leif other than the brief conversations yesterday and today.

"I brought the schedule for class and what all is expected in this course. I have one week before the first speech is due and it needs to be on something I feel strongly about."

Okay. I was a tutor. I could do this. He was just another student who needed my help. "So, we need to decide what you're passionate about." He chuckled and I glanced up from his syllabus. "What?" I asked, when I saw his amused expression.

"What I'm passionate about?"

I rolled my eyes and held up the syllabus. "You know, something you feel strongly about. Like your purpose or platform."

He nodded with his amused grin still in place. "Passionate, I like that. Let's think of something I'm passionate about."

This one shouldn't take him long to figure out. Some football topic or sports related issue had to be swirling around in his head. I reached over to open the notebook. "Got any ideas?" I asked.

He appeared deep in thought. It surprised me a little. How deep could one get when it came to football? "The importance of adoption."

I started to write down his answer as his words slowly sank in. Adoption? He wanted to write about adoption? "Okay," I replied wondering if he would elaborate on why he wanted to discuss this. I completely agreed with him, but how could Mr. Popular be passionate about something so important?

He studied the pencil in his hand and flipped it back and forth between his fingers. I could tell he was deciding on how to explain to me why he wanted to write about adoption. So I managed to keep my mouth shut and wait. Finally he glanced up at me. "I was adopted after living in foster homes for five years. I'd given up hope that I would get a family by the time I turned nine because most people want babies. I was given a chance most nine year old foster kids only dream of."

If he'd just spoke to me in fluent Chinese I wouldn't have been more shocked. Adopted? Leif Montgomery? Really? "Oh, wow, I had no idea. I, uh, can see why this would be an important topic for you." When I'd said I didn't know Leif Montgomery, I hadn't realized how accurate my words were. The little boy in a foster home with no parents and a learning disability didn't seem to fit the guy who walked the halls of Harbor High as the reigning king. The things about Leif I disliked now seemed like impressive accomplishments. Was it possible I'd labeled him incorrectly? Shallow jocks didn't overcome adversity and accomplish the things Leif had. I'd labeled him, not even knowing him. Just because girls went gaga over him and every boy wanted to be him didn't make him a jerk. The only jerk in the room happened to be the judgmental, elitist female. Me.

"You did hear the part where I got adopted, right?" His voice broke into my thoughts and I glanced up at him confused. A grin tugged at his lips. "You look so distraught. I thought maybe you missed the happy ending."

"I'm sorry. It's just, well, I wasn't expecting that. You kind of surprised me."

He leaned back in his chair. "It sure seems to me that you have a lot of ideas where I'm concerned. You sure have put a lot of thought into someone you don't like very much."

My face grew warm and I knew I was turning a brilliant shade of red. "Who knows Pagan, you may like me before this is over."


It took us three consecutive nights of tutoring to get his speech ready. It also only took three nights for me to realize I really liked Harbor High's star quarterback. Leif Montgomery was nothing like I'd always assumed. I still felt guilty over the stereotype I'd placed on him. However, just because we were spending two hours together every evening, nothing changed at school. Though Leif smiled and nodded when we passed in the halls, we didn't carry the easy friendship we seemed to have during tutoring into our daily life at school.

"K, sooooo, here's the thing, Wyatt and I have been talking some and he ask me to the Homecoming Dance. And that means you're going to have to get a date and come too. I know we planned to go to the movies that night but welllll...." Miranda batted her eyelashes at me from across the table.

"I'm thrilled you and Wyatt are making up. I hated having the two of you mad at each other."

"Me too. It sucked, didn't it?" Wyatt chimed in, as he took the seat beside Miranda. She beamed over at him and I suddenly felt a little left out.

"And Pagan needs a date to the dance. We can't go without her." Miranda said grinning at Wyatt.

"I am pretty sure Pagan can get a date if she wants one." He took a bite of his hamburger. I knew he intended to do his best to rein in Miranda's match-making ideas. I flashed him a grateful smile.

"There isn't anyone I really want to go with." This was a lie and I knew it. I forced myself not to look at Leif's table because doing so would give me away. Wyatt, however, glanced over at Leif's table and back at me with a smirk. Thankfully Miranda missed his subtle hint and Wyatt decided not to verbalize his thoughts. Miranda picking up on my interest in Leif was the last thing I needed.

"But it won't be fun without you," Miranda pouted. I took another drink of my tea. I didn't want to argue with her about this. "Come on, Pagan, it has been like six months since Jay left. We miss him, too, but he moved away. You need to date again."

It was the first time the mention of my former boyfriend didn't make me sad. I'd started dating him my ninth grade year and he'd been a junior. After graduation this past May he left for college and his parents moved to another state. We both agreed a long distance relationship would be too hard and we broke up. At first, I'd been lost. I'd assumed it must be a broken heart. It didn't take me long to realize I missed the comfort of our relationship. Deep down, we'd just been really good friends. We liked the same things and cared about the same things

"It isn't because of Jay. I just haven't met anyone else who interests me."

Wyatt's grin got bigger as he took another bite of his burger. If he wasn't careful I would strangle that goofy grin off his face.

Miranda sighed in exasperation. "It's a pity you spend every evening with Leif Montgomery and you don't even like him. I just don't get it."

Wyatt raised his eyebrows at her and frowned. "What are you saying, Miranda?"

She puckered her lips and tried to look serious. "Oh, stop it, Wyatt, you know I love you." He bent down and gave her a peck on the lips before returning to his food. She turned her attention back to me with a silly grin on her face and I wanted to laugh. "I'm just saying if you could get past your dislike for him it would be a prime opportunity."

I thought for a minute about continuing to let her think I really disliked Leif. Somehow it seemed unfair to Leif. He didn't deserve my dislike and letting others think I didn't like him was wrong.

"I don't dislike Leif. He isn't like what I thought. I was wrong about him. However, I'm also not hot after him. " I glanced up from my tray half afraid Miranda might have managed to read between the lines but instead she looked like a deer caught in the headlights. She wasn't focused on me, her gaze was locked on something or someone behind me.

"Well, I'm glad to know you're not hot after me. One less worry on my mind."

I closed my eyes tightly, hoping I'd just imagined Leif's voice. His shoulder brushed mine as he sat down beside me and I slowly opened my eyes to see a very amused Wyatt watching me. I cleared my throat and forced a smile I didn't feel, before turning to look at Leif.

"Hi," I said simply and he chuckled, nudging my shoulder with his arm.

"Relax, Pagan, it's okay. I'm aware you used to hate my guts and have had a realization from the gods that I'm not so bad after all. It's cool." I resisted the desire to sigh in relief.

"So, what brings you to the lower class tables?" Wyatt asked, grinning at his own humor.

Leif glanced over at him and raised an eyebrow in surprise. "Oh, you mean this is lower class? I had no idea. It has the star athlete being scouted by colleges," he motioned to Wyatt, "his girlfriend," motioning to Miranda, "and last year's homecoming queen," he said, turning to me.

I rolled my eyes, "That was only because of my date and you know it."

"No, I don't know it."

I knew I was blushing and I hated it. My gaze met Miranda's and I realized she was soaking in every word. This wasn't good. She wouldn't miss my pink cheeks. "What is it you need?" I asked, trying not to sound rude.

He grinned as if he could read my mind. "I wanted to tell you I got an A on my speech."

"That's wonderful. It's a really good speech. You had some great stuff in it."

"Yes, but I couldn't have done it without your help."

I smiled and stared back down at my food. I hadn't told anyone, Miranda included, about Leif's dyslexia or his adoption. Those weren't my stories to tell.

"Are you coming to the game tonight?" he asked, and I glanced back up at him, surprised by his question.

"Um, no, probably not."

He frowned, and then nodded and stood up. "Well, thanks again, and I guess I'll see you Monday, then."

"Okay. Good luck tonight," I replied. Had it hurt his feelings that I wasn't going to the game? I turned back around in my seat and Wyatt shook his head.

"What?" I asked.

"Poor guy isn't use to being shot down," he said and took a swig of his milk.

"Shot down?" I asked, confused. He sat his carton back down on his tray and stared at me with a serious expression, one rarely seen on Wyatt's face.

"He wanted you to come to his game and you said no."

I frowned trying to remember if he'd asked me to come. I felt positive he'd asked me if I planned on coming. Not once did he ask me to come. "No he didn't."

Wyatt chuckled and shook his head. "Dating Jay ruined you. Most of the time people don't date someone just exactly like them. You understood Jay because, like you, he was straight-forward and serious. Not all guys, no, make that most guys, are not like that." He nodded toward where Leif stood talking to Kendra. "He was asking, trust me." Wyatt walked off and I glanced back at Leif.

Kendra twirled her long blond hair around her finger while grinning up at him. Just a week ago, I would've thought he deserved someone so superficial and beautiful. Now, I knew better. He glanced up and caught me watching him. His eyes seemed to say something I didn't understand but before I could figure it out they changed and took on a polite expression. He turned his attention back to Kendra. Confused and a little annoyed, I grabbed my tray and started to stand up. I started to tell Miranda I'd see her later when I realized she was staring at me with her mouth slightly open.

"What?" I asked, a little defensively, because I knew by the expression on her face that she'd figured it out.

"You...like....him," she said slowly as in amazement.

I rolled my eyes and laughed. "Not hardly." I grabbed my tray and headed to the garbage and away from Miranda's knowing eyes.


"Do girls your age not normally go out and do things on the weekend?" This time I was unable to stop the startled scream that erupted out of my mouth. Luckily my mom wasn't home to hear me. I spun around to find the talking soul sitting on my bed watching me.

"Would you PLEASE stop popping up out of nowhere and scaring the bejesus out of me! And what are you doing in my room? Go away!" I threw the shirt I'd been about to hang up in my closet at him for good measure. This was getting old. He needed to stop following me around.

One of his dark eyebrows lifted. "You aren't normally so testy."

Growling loudly, I stalked over to my window, opened it, and then turned back to him. "Fly away please. Stay out of my room. I could have been naked!"

A deep chuckle caused a strange warmth to course through my body. Dizziness seemed to touch me but just barely. "You want me to fly away? That's cute."

I didn't want to be cute but I also couldn't seem to work up a good mad anymore either. Some strange lethargy had come over me. Had his laugh caused this relaxing warmth in my body?

"No, not exactly, but I do have the ability to control anxiety or panic. My laugh didn't really have anything to do with it."

Did he just read my thoughts or had I said that out loud? He seemed to find me amusing if the smirk on his face was any indication. Another reason I should be furious with him. Stupid talking dead guy.

"For what it's worth I'm sorry I scared you. It wasn't my intention, but if I'd appeared in front of you standing in your closet would that have been less frightening?"

I thought about him popping up in front of me and a small laugh escaped my lips. He was right. I'd have probably fainted. But he could have tried knocking or something. Wait, could ghosts knock or would their fists just go through the door?

"I see your point," I replied and started to close the window, and then decided against it. It made me feel safer with it open. "Why are you here?" I asked.

"Why are you here?" he replied. Did the guy get off on talking in riddles?

"I live here."

He shrugged. "Yes, but you're young. You have friends. It's the weekend. I know they're out having a good time so why are you here?"

Great, the talking soul wants to be nosey now. "I'm not in the mood to go out."

"Because of the football player?"

What did he know about Leif? I walked over and sat down in the plush chair I kept in the far corner of my room for reading. Apparently, I was going to have to talk to the guy in order to get him to leave. "Not really, mostly because I don't want to be Miranda and Wyatt's third wheel."

"But she keeps calling and inviting you to go places with them. Sounds to me like she wants you around."

How did he know she'd called me? I sat up straight and tucked my feet under me, trying to get some anger worked up at his sneaking around but I couldn't. "Have you been watching me?" I asked studying his expression for any sign of a lie.

He flashed me a wicked grin, tucked his hands behind his head, and laid back. "For weeks, Pagan, for weeks."

Weeks? I opened my mouth and then closed it not sure what to say. Had he seen me naked? Did I really want to know if he had? How had he hid from me? Was he in my room when I was sleeping? I shook my head trying to clear the questions racing to mind.

"I'll see you later. Your mother's home." I jerked my gaze up from my hands, which I'd been wringing in my lap nervously, but my bed was empty.

"PAGAN! Come help me get the groceries inside!" Mom called from the bottom of the stairs. I sighed and stood up, glancing back once more to my empty bed before running downstairs to help her unload the car.

Sleep did not come easy the rest of the weekend. I'd even slept with my door open and my closet light on. It was ridiculous that he had me scared of the dark. The dark circles under my eyes had been impossible to completely cover this morning. Tugging my book bag up higher on my shoulder, I made my way through the packed hallway. I passed Leif and he nodded politely. The other times I'd seen him today, he hadn't even noticed me. Why his lack of attention made me want to go back home and crawl in bed I didn't know. But then again I may just want to go crawl in bed because sexy-dead-stalker-dude was causing me to lose sleep and I was exhausted.

"Don't look at him next time. It'll drive him crazy." The familiar drawl didn't startle me. It was almost as if I expected him. Even though he'd been frustratingly absent since telling me he'd been watching me for weeks Saturday afternoon. Of course, there was no way I could respond to him right now and he knew it. I turned and headed for my locker. "He's trying to play hard to get. Kind of proves what a child he is, but I can see it's bothering you."

"I'm not bothered," I said between my teeth as I opened my locker.

"Yes, you are. There is this little wrinkle between your eyebrows that appears and you nibble your bottom lip when something bothers you."

I knew I didn't need to look at him but I couldn't help it. I turned my head and peered at him through my hair. He was leaning against the locker beside mine with his arms crossed over his chest, watching me. No one had ever paid enough attention to me before to actually be able to describe my facial expression when I was bothered. It was oddly endearing.

"You're missing the public display of affection across the hall between your two buddies. They may need you to throw a bucket of ice water on them." I bit my lip to keep from laughing. I didn't need to turn around to know what he was talking about. Miranda and Wyatt could be a little gross. "There that's better. I like it when you're smiling. If the football kid keeps making you frown I'm going to take matters into my own hands." I opened my mouth to protest but he was gone.


I glanced over at the clock. Leif would be here any minute. My mother had left thirty minutes ago for another date with Roger. I'd spent the time alone walking through the house looking for the soul I couldn't seem to get rid of. I wasn't sure where I expected to find him. He didn't really seem to be the kind of guy who sits around and does nothing. If he was here wouldn't he be trying to tell me what to do or asking me questions that were none of his business? But I searched for him anyway. I wanted to discuss the comment he made earlier. The doorbell interrupted my hunt and I headed back to the living room to get the door.

"Hey." I stepped back and let Leif in. I'd ignored him the rest of the day. Wasn't sure what good it did, but I decided I didn't want Leif thinking I cared if he spoke to me or not.

"Hey," he replied and stepped inside. I led him over to the kitchen table and waited while he set his books down.

"Safe sex," he announced.

I froze and stared at him, unsure whether I'd just heard him correctly. His serious face broke into a grin and then he started laughing.

"I wish you could see your face," he said through his fits of laughter.

"You did say 'safe sex' then?" I asked, trying to determine what was so funny. He was the one talking about sex.

He nodded and held up his paper. "The topic for this week's speech."

I laughed weakly. "Okay, well that was one way to announce it," I replied while going to the fridge to get our drinks.

"I'm hoping you're well educated on this topic because I haven't got a clue."

"What?" I squeaked in reply.

He laughed again and I stood there waiting on him to get a grip. "I'm sorry," he said, "It's just that you're so cute when you're shocked."

I stiffened at the word cute and wished I hadn't. Hoping he didn't notice my reaction, I took a deep breath and prayed silently for my eyes not to betray me when I turned around. It wasn't as if I wanted Leif to see me differently but I didn't exactly want him to think I was cute. Maybe attractive or pretty, even, but not cute. Although him referring to me as cute helped remind me where I stood with him. Any delusions I may have had of us being anything other than friends dissipated.

"I think having had actual experience isn't necessary. It's basically supposed to be about your beliefs on the subject or the importance of it." I couldn't bring myself to meet his eyes.

He reached over and tilted my chin up so I wouldn't have a choice. "You're embarrassed." I averted my eyes and he chuckled. "That's cute."

Ugh! We were back to me being cute. I glanced back at him. "Please stop saying I'm cute. It's kind of insulting."

He frowned as he dropped his hand from my chin. "How is that insulting?"

I shrugged, not wanting to talk about it and wishing I'd kept my mouth shut. "It just is. No one wants to be cute. Puppies are cute." I reached for his notebook and kept my eyes on the paper and read over the topic, or at least attempted to act like I was reading over it.

"Well, you definitely don't look like a puppy," he said with a chuckle.

"Well, that's something at least." We needed to change the subject and I needed to learn to curb my tongue.

"Okay, so what are the three main reasons you believe safe sex is important?" Maybe now we could get off the topic of me and my cuteness. He didn't answer and I glanced up at him. He was watching me with a serious expression.

"Are you not sure?"

He didn't reply.

"Um, okay what about teenage pregnancy? That's a good point. No one needs to become a parent while they're still a kid."

Again, he didn't respond, so I wrote it down.

"Your feelings are hurt," he said quietly. I froze but kept my eyes on the paper. "I didn't mean to say something to hurt your feelings," he continued.

I wanted to deny it but I figured accepting his apology and moving on would be the best way to handle this. "It's fine. Let's get working on your essay."

He stared down at the paper. "Teenage pregnancy is definitely one reason," he agreed.

"Okay, so what about STD's?" I suggested, writing it down as I spoke.

"That's another good one."

I started to write it down but he reached over and took the notebook from me. Startled, I jerked my head up to see what he was doing. He gave me an apologetic smile. "Sorry, but I couldn't think of any other way to get your attention."

Not sure how to respond, I sat silently and waited on him to finish.

"You aren't just cute. Yes, you make cute faces and do cute things but you aren't just cute." Hearing him explain himself made me feel silly for even saying anything about it.

"Okay," I managed to mumble.

He slid the notebook back to me. "Now, let's see...what about the fact that using a condom takes away from the pleasure, should we discuss that?"

I choked on my soda and started coughing uncontrollably while Leif patted me on the back. Once I got myself under control, I glanced up and caught him biting back a smile.

"Again, you do a lot of cute things, but you aren't just cute."

# Chapter Four

Leif didn't show up last night to finish his speech and it was due today. Not showing up wasn't like him. The later it got without a call from him the angrier I'd become. In the end, I finished the speech myself and printed it out. Deep down I believed he would have a good excuse and letting him make a bad grade had seemed cruel. I reached into my bag to pull out his speech as I made my way down the hall. I just hoped when I found him and handed him this paper he would have a legitimate excuse for last night. Admitting to myself that I needed him to have a really good excuse hadn't been easy. I'd let myself care about Leif Montgomery way too much.

"Hey girly, what's up? I miss you." Miranda slipped her arm around my waist and laid her head on my shoulder. I missed her too. Last year when she and Wyatt had been dating I'd been with Jay. It hadn't made me feel isolated from my friends when they'd become an item. With me being single and the other two in my trio being a couple, I couldn't help but feel like the third wheel.

"I miss you too. We need to go out together one night. Maybe a girls' night out," I suggested while searching through the crowd of students clogging up the hallway for Leif.

"That sounds wonderful! Let's plan on doing it one night this weekend." She paused and frowned. "Or maybe next weekend." The uncharacteristic frown was proof enough she hated telling me she was busy.

I shrugged and forced a smile. "No worries. Whenever you have time." I glanced back down the hall and this time managed to get a glimpse of Leif at his locker. His back faced the crowded hallway. I turned back to Miranda. "I need to get this to Leif. I'll catch up with you at lunch."

The crowd seemed to thin out as I reached his end of the lockers. Once I broke through the last group of students standing between us, I noticed Kendra leaning against his locker, smiling up at him. I thought about turning around, not wanting to hand this to him in front of her when I remembered he went to Speech first period. I slowed down and stopped behind him. As I reached to tap him on the shoulder, Kendra reached up and ran her fingers through Leif's hair. It was sickening to watch. He was such a good guy and she was pure evil.

"You sure coming over last night wasn't a big deal? I would hate to mess things up with you and your girlfriend," she cooed.

"You know she isn't my girlfriend, Kendra. Stop calling her that. You'll start talk." His voice sounded annoyed. Was the idea that someone might think he liked me so repulsive to him? A sick knot formed in my stomach and I started to turn and leave before he noticed me.

"You spend a lot of time at her house and she is always looking at you."

"She's my tutor and no, she isn't looking at me. You're just being paranoid when you have no reason to be."

I clinched my empty hand into a fist thinking about all the times he had fooled me into thinking he was a nice guy. He was just as mean and calculating as Kendra. Was he even adopted or had that been a big elaborate lie to get me to feel sorry for him? I'd actually convinced my stupid self that Leif might be potential relationship material. The next time he came to my lunch table and asked if I was going to go to his game, I had intended to say yes and see if it led to where Wyatt had seemed to think it was leading.

"You sure she knows she isn't your girlfriend because it looks like she is stalking you?" Kendra purred. I turned back around hating the heat I felt in my cheeks. My face was probably bright red.

"Oh, uh, Pagan. I was going to come find you and explain about last night." I nodded, not wanting to discuss this after all I'd heard, and handed him the paper. "Thought you might need this."

He stared down at the paper in my hand before reaching out and taking it. I turned to walk away. "Wait, I was going to call you last night. I just got tied up. Thanks," he said holding up the paper.

Kendra slipped an arm inside his and smiled sweetly up at him. "That's not true, Leif, I never tied you up." She then directed her gaze at me and gave me a smile of triumph. While I'd sat up late finishing his speech, he'd been with Kendra. How stupid could I be? I'd wasted my time writing a speech for someone who I'd thought needed my help, all this time thinking he was a good guy I could, possibly, really like. Maybe I hadn't judged him so unfairly before. Maybe Leif Montgomery fit the description I'd placed on him all these years. It hurt to find out the guy I'd built him up to be was an illusion. That I'd made an idiot of myself by staying up and writing the paper for him. It made me look like one his love-struck groupies.

I managed to get my locker open and find the books I needed for first class through my haze of anger. I stopped, closed my eyes, and took a deep breath. I'd just learned a lesson and I didn't need to forget it. Two tears squeezed through and I quickly wiped them away before closing my locker door. Now he had me crying. Perfect.

"Pagan."

Crap! He'd come after me. I couldn't let him see me crying. Humiliation wouldn't be a strong enough word for what I'd feel if Leif knew I'd shed a tear over this. I forced a nonchalant expression on my face and turned around. "Yes?"

He appeared upset. I wished I could convince myself of his sincerity. "Look, about last night, I am really sorry. I hadn't expected you to finish the speech for me. I messed up and I was going to take the bad grade. I should've called, but—"

I shook my head to stop him. "It's not a big deal. However, from now on would you please let me know in advance when you won't be able to make it to the appointed time for your session? Now, if you'll excuse me." I stepped around him and started for class.

"Pagan, wait, please."

I stopped and considered telling him to go to Hell but decided against it before turning back to face him. "What?"

"I was coming over and Kendra called."

I shook my head. "I don't care. Just call next time, please." I turned and headed toward my class but when I reached it, I didn't stop walking. Going into a classroom late with everyone's eyes on me didn't seem possible at that moment.

I opened the front door of the school and stepped outside. I normally didn't put myself out there for anyone. Today I'd made the mistake of doing so and got burned. I just wanted to go home. I could deal with my wounded pride alone.

"Don't leave. He isn't worth it." The familiar deep voice almost sounded as if he were pleading. He was walking beside me. His face was tense and the smirk I'd grown accustomed to was missing.

"I don't want to stay. I'm angry and I just want to leave."

"Please, Pagan, don't get in your car. Go back inside. Forget the stupid kid and enjoy the rest of your day. Don't let something that idiot did send you running."

I stopped walking and looked at him. "Why do you care if I leave? Are you the new hall monitor and I missed the memo?"

His frown deepened; blue eyes turning icy blue as if a fire had ignited behind them. "I'm begging you to go back in the school."

"Why?" He ran his hand through his dark, silky hair and growled in frustration. "Do you have to question everything? Can't you just listen for once?"

That was it. I'd had more than enough for one day. First Leif proves he's a grade-A jerk, and then the soul who won't leave me alone decides to get annoyed with me. "I'm leaving here. You can't stop me. I don't have to listen to you. If you don't have a good excuse then there is no reason for me to stay." I twirled around on the balls of my feet and stalked to my car. Guys were annoying, alive or dead, it didn't seem to matter.

I quickly cranked the car and focused on getting out of the school parking lot. I didn't want anyone to see me and report me before I could get out of here. I couldn't believe I'd actually shed a tear over this. Crying wasn't my thing. It had to have been the humiliation. I wasn't accustomed to it and obviously didn't know how to deal with it.

I adjusted the rear view mirror to see if I looked as bad as I feared, in case my mother came out of her writing burrow when I got home. If my mascara was smeared my mother would notice. I wouldn't be able to hide the frustration. Fake smiles weren't a talent of mine.

Sighing, I glanced back at the road. Attempting to fix my face without the help of soap and water was a hopeless cause. The stop sign I'd stopped at a million times surprised me. I hadn't been paying attention and I'd forgotten to slow down. It was too late to slam on the breaks. I glanced over just in time to see a truck coming directly at me and in one split second the realization hit me: I wouldn't be able to stop in time.

Everything went black and the screeching wheels and honking horn fell silent. A spinning sensation and a sharp pain shot through my body. I tried to scream for help but nothing came out. I began suffocating. Something heavy was pressed against my chest and I couldn't breathe. I gasped and reached into the darkness for help. I would suffocate if I didn't get the heavy weight off my chest. I fought to open my eyes but the darkness held me under. Warmth spread over me as I grabbed something in the darkness. I froze, not sure what I'd found when I realized I could breathe again. The lights suddenly came back on and the world became blindingly bright. I couldn't open my eyes because of the pain. Someone carried me a short distance and then I felt the cool ground under my back. The abnormally warm hands cradling me disappeared. I tried to protest. I didn't want my rescuer to leave me, but I couldn't find my voice. I tried to sit up and intense pain overtook my body. The world went silent.

A hauntingly sweet sound played in the darkness. I turned my head to find the source of the music. My neck was stiff and my head began pounding so loudly it dulled the sound of the melody I'd been trying to find. I stopped moving and kept my eyes closed, waiting for the pain to stop.

"And she awakes," a voice said in the darkness. I recognized it and instead of fearing it the sound soothed me. The music started playing again and I realized it was the soft strum of a guitar. A low hum joined in and I lay still, listening in the darkness, and glad that the music filled the void, assuring me I wasn't alone.

Needing to see him, I opened my eyes and realized the lights were off. I lay still while my eyes adjusted to the dark room. I wasn't in my bedroom. The machine beside me and the needle in my arm were the only clues I needed. I was in a hospital room. The guitar stopped playing. Afraid to turn my head again, I carefully shifted my body instead.

The soul sat in a dark corner, watching me. "What are you doing?" I managed to ask in a hoarse whisper.

He smiled, stood up, and walked over to me. "Well, I'd have thought it would've been obvious." He held up the guitar in his hands. Not only could this soul speak, he also played musical instruments. I wanted to ask more but my throat hurt too badly. He sat down in a chair someone had pulled up beside my bed. "You probably don't need to talk. You were in a car accident and you've suffered a serious concussion along with a broken rib. Other than that, you're just badly bruised up."

I remembered the stop sign, and the truck had been coming at me too fast. I'd known it would be unable to stop in time.

"You were wearing your seat-belt and the truck hit the back end of your car and it flipped you a few times."

Did my mom know? She would be terrified. How long had it been? And why was a soul the only person with me? I glanced over to the machine my wires were hooked up to and, if I were reading it correctly, then I was indeed alive. The sudden fear at the prospect I might be dead eased and I stared back into those intense dark blue eyes.

"Mom?" I managed to ask through my dry sore throat.

The soul smiled. "She just stepped out for some coffee a few moments ago. I expect her to be returning soon enough."

Mom was here and I would see her in a few minutes. I felt like a little girl, afraid of the dark. Tears stung my eyes as I glanced toward the door, hoping it would open to reveal my mother. A woman with short brown, curly hair drifted into my room without the use of the door. I studied her and she smiled at me but gazed right past the other soul in the room. Once, when I was ten, I had been put in the hospital for pneumonia and I'd realized then that lost, wandering souls were in abundance inside hospitals. This one drifted over to some flowers I hadn't noticed before by the window. She seemed to be smelling them and she gave a gentle tug to the bunch of 'Get Well' balloons attached to a dozen yellow daisies. I glanced back at the soul who sat beside me. He seemed to be studying me intently.

"You see her, don't you?" he asked, and I nodded. He watched the lady as she glanced back at me one more time before drifting back through the wall. "Have you always seen them?"

I managed to smile at the way he referred to souls as if he was not one himself. I raised my eyebrows and stared at him pointedly. "You're one of them," I said in a whisper.

"Yes, I guess, to you, it would seem that way. However, there is a difference between souls and me."

I frowned. "What?" I knew he could talk to me and souls never spoke to me but he was still a soul without a body.

"I can't tell you what I am. I've broken enough rules already." He studied the machine beside me instead of meeting my gaze. The door to my room opened and my mother walked in.

Her eyes found mine and she gasped before running over to me, "Pagan, you're awake! Oh, honey, I'm so sorry I wasn't here when you woke up. All alone and confused in a dark hospital room."

I peeked behind her and saw the soul standing there watching with the sexy smirk I was beginning to get attached to on his perfect lips.

"I just needed a little coffee and then I ran to get this magazine," she said holding up a plastic green bag. "Let me get the nurse. You just be still. You're a little busted up but you're going to be okay." Tears sprang to her eyes and she covered her mouth with her hand. "I'm sorry," she said gazing down at me with watery eyes. "It's just,

I keep thinking about your car and how it would have completely crushed you if you hadn't been thrown from the driver's seat. I always tell you to wear your seat-belt and the fact you didn't listen to me saved your life." She let out a small sob and smiled apologetically at me. "Oh, baby, I'm just so glad you have opened your eyes."

I smiled at her trying to mask my confusion. "It's okay," I whispered.

She bent down and kissed my forehead. "I'll be right back. I need to get a nurse. They've been waiting for you to wake up."

She headed for the door and I stared back at the soul standing in the corner with the guitar in his hand. It struck me as odd to see him hold a guitar. Did people see a guitar floating in the air? Mom hadn't seemed to notice, but then she hadn't looked anywhere but at me.

"The seat-belt," I whispered through my dry lips. I'd been wearing my seat-belt. I always did. He'd even said it was a good thing I was wearing it. Why did my mother think I hadn't been, and that not wearing it had saved my life? He stepped forward, watching me closely. The expression on his face said he didn't know how to answer me. Before he could reply, the door opened again and he retreated back to the corner. A nurse came bustling in with my mother behind her. The answer to my question would have to wait.

The soul left before the nurse finished with me and he hadn't returned. The next time I woke up I quickly checked around the room, hoping he'd come back, but my mother now sat in his corner working on her laptop. She gazed over at me and smiled.

"Good morning!" The fear I'd seen in her eyes last night was gone...she looked less tense and more like my mom again. Now that I'd awakened and the nurse had assured her I would recover just fine, she seemed less tense and more like my mom again.

I smiled. "Morning." My throat felt a bit better thanks to all the ice cubes I'd eaten. I reached for my cup of water and Mom jumped up quickly.

"Don't move. Your broken rib is going to require that you be still for a while." She put the straw to my lips and I took small sips of the cold water. It felt wonderful on my sore throat. "Miranda has already called this morning and I told her you woke up last night. She is on her way, with Wyatt," Mom paused and glanced back at the door, "and Leif Montgomery has been in the waiting room all night. He even slept in there. I went and let him know you'd woken up and I told him to go on home because you couldn't have visitors, but he stayed. The nurses felt bad for him and gave him a pillow and blankets." She trailed off as if not sure exactly why he'd wanted to stay in a waiting room all night. The memories of his not showing up for our study session because of Kendra resurfaced. I didn't feel sad anymore or disappointed. The tears I'd shed over him had been pointless.

Mom chewed on her bottom lip. "He said he was the reason you left school upset. I haven't asked you why you weren't at school or what happened because I didn't want to upset you." She stopped talking and studied me, waiting for me to say something. What could I say? I really didn't want to see Leif. I'd almost killed myself acting like a silly girl with a crush.

"He's been here all night?" I asked, wanting to make sure I understood her correctly.

She nodded. "He's been here since he found out about your accident. He came with Miranda and Wyatt, but he wouldn't leave with them."

"Okay, um, if he wants to come in, then that's fine."

Mom appeared relieved. I guess she'd worried I might tell the poor boy who'd waited all night in an uncomfortable waiting room that I didn't want to see him. She hurried out the door and I heard Miranda whisper something as they passed each other. No doubt they were discussing my agreeing to let Leif in to see me. Miranda walked inside and put her hands on her hips and gave me a big cheery smile.

"Look at you, all awake and gorgeous," she said, walking over to me and sitting in the chair beside the bed. She grabbed my hand and I saw the glistening in her eyes as she fought off tears. I squeezed her hand and her bravado cracked. She let out a sob as tears started running down her face. I glanced up at Wyatt, who stood behind her watching me. He shrugged and gave me what I could tell was a forced smile.

Miranda choked on a sob. "I'm sorry. I said I wasn't going to cry. I really had myself all worked up to be bright and cheery but I keep remembering your car and hearing the words 'she was rushed to the hospital unconscious' over and over again in my head." She wiped her wet face and smiled through her tears. "I'm just so glad you're okay. Yesterday was the worst day of my life." She took our joined hands up to her mouth and kissed them.

"I know," I said simply. Because I did. If it had been her in this bed instead of me I would've been terrified.

"Ironic isn't it. The one day you decide to break the rules and skip school and not wear your seat belt, which is weird since you're the Seat Belt Nazi, it all blows up in your face. Makes you want to keep walking the straight and narrow doesn't it?" Wyatt asked with a grin on his face.

I smiled because laughing hurt, and Miranda rolled her eyes but a smile tugged on the corner her mouth. "Yes, I guess so." I wanted to clarify the fact I'd been wearing my seat belt but I couldn't explain something I didn't understand, so I kept my mouth shut. A knock sounded on the door and Miranda stared at me, chewing her bottom lip nervously.

She lowered her voice to a whisper. "He hasn't left since he got here with us yesterday. He even missed football practice."

I watched as Leif walked inside the room. His eyes met mine and he paused a moment before walking into the room farther. I wasn't sure exactly what to say to him or what he could possibly say to me. He was a guy I tutored and he'd slept in the waiting room all night because I'd acted ridiculous over his blowing off our study session. He was obviously nervous and I knew Wyatt and Miranda's presence wasn't helping matters. I didn't intend to tell everyone my accident was his fault. I didn't believe that. I knew I'd caused this. Letting him off the hook would be easy enough. However, with my two best friends in the room it would be awkward. I didn't want them to leave me because having them here felt like a security blanket. I glanced back at Leif and I could see in his eyes he wanted to talk to me without the audience but he wouldn't ask them to leave. The thought of him sleeping in the waiting room all night because he felt guilty seemed unfair. I needed to ease his conscious so he could go home.

I turned to Miranda and Wyatt. "Could you two give us a minute?"

Miranda glared over at Leif and nodded. I watched as she stood up. Staring at Leif wasn't something new for Miranda but glaring at him was. After I rectified the situation with Leif I would need to clear things up with my friends as well. Once the door closed behind them, I turned my attention to him.

"Yesterday, I.... God." He ran his hand through his messy, blond hair and closed his eyes. "You're here because of me. I know you left because you were upset. I could see it in your eyes but I didn't know how to make you talk to me." He stopped again and gazed down at me. "I can never express to you how sorry I am."

I shook my head. "This wasn't your fault. I made a stupid decision."

"No, it is my fault. I could see the tears in your eyes, Pagan, and it was killing me but I couldn't find the right words. I wanted to explain but I did a poor job."

I couldn't let him take the blame for my stupidity. "Stop blaming yourself. I will admit that I acted foolishly over you not showing up or calling. I did let the fact you were with Kendra upset me and that was silly. I don't know why I let it upset me like it did. Crying over a guy isn't something I do. The fact I was fighting back tears confused me and I left."

He reached out and gently touched one of the two dozen pink roses sitting on a table by the window. "You left because I hurt you. That makes this my fault," he replied simply. I didn't want him beating himself up over this. He needed to get over it and go home.

"Leif, I'm your tutor. We aren't even friends. You can miss a session and forget to call me, and I shouldn't let that hurt me. I read more into our relationship than I should have. You have never insinuated we were more than study partners. We don't speak at school; we don't see each other except at my house when we are working. This was my fault. Stop blaming yourself and go home." I said the last with a softness to my voice so it didn't sound rude. He frowned and walked over to stand beside my bed.

"You think I only see you as my tutor?" he asked. I nodded, unsure of his meaning. He gave me a sad smirk. "That would be my fault too. I have never had a problem letting a girl know I'm interested...until you." I wasn't sure what he meant so I remained silent. He sat down in the chair Miranda vacated moments ago.

"I knew you didn't like me when you agreed to tutor me. You didn't have to tell me that day in the hall when you said you'd turned me down because you didn't like me. I've always known you didn't like me, but I wanted you to be my tutor. I wanted you to be the one to know my secret. Never did I expect the one girl who looked at me with disdain would be so much fun. It came as a surprise to find out the girl I'd been watching since our freshman year in high school happened to be just as beautiful on the inside as she was on the outside. You surprised me and it didn't take much to hook me." A sad smile touched his lips. "Yet, at school you still seemed as untouchable as always, so I kept my distance. I tried speaking to you and even got up the nerve to ask you out but your disinterest scared me. I didn't want to make our nights together uncomfortable, so I didn't ask for anything more. I looked forward to our nights all day long. I couldn't mess those up."

He dropped his gaze down to his hands, which he'd fisted in his lap. "Then Kendra called and she started crying, saying she needed to talk to someone and I was the only person she trusted. I told her I had somewhere to be but she cried harder and begged me. I agreed to stop by her house. She is dealing with some things in her home life that I already knew about and she needed someone to listen. When I realized I wasn't going to be able to leave her, I wanted to call but I couldn't call you in front of her and explain it. So, I didn't. I was just going to deal with the bad grade. I had no idea you would even care." He glanced up at me with a pained expression on his face. "I was wrong and I've never been so mad at myself." He stood, shoving his hands in his jeans pockets with a look of defeat on his face.

I smiled. "Please don't be mad at yourself. I don't blame you for anything." I wanted to say more but I couldn't. He watched me a moment before nodding.

"Is there a chance I haven't completely screwed things up between us?" he asked.

"What is it you're worried about screwing up? I'll still tutor you, if that's what you're asking."

He chuckled softly and gently took my hand. "I'm really grateful that you'll remain my tutor but that isn't what I'm asking. I was scared before of messing things up but I don't think I can mess anything up any more than I already have." He sat back down in the chair beside me and gazed at me with baby blue eyes that were framed in such thick lashes it made it hard not to sigh. "I don't want you to just be my tutor. I want you to be the girl I look for in the halls every morning and save a seat for in the cafeteria. I want you to be the one waiting for me when I walk off the field at my games. I want you to be the one I pick up the phone to call just to make me smile." His eyes watched me. Leif Montgomery actually appeared nervous.

He was waiting for me to say something. I could see the question in his eyes. Leif wanted to take this to a level I'd thought I wanted before, so why was it so hard to accept now? Fear flickered in his eyes and I managed to nod my head. I'd agreed to let things change between us, but somehow, deep down, something didn't feel right.

# Chapter Five

I remained in the hospital for an entire week. Every night, I went to sleep to the gentle strum of a guitar. When I would wake in the middle of the night it was never to an empty hospital room but to the dark, mysterious soul I'd grown attached to. He sat in the shadows and played a lullaby I'd decided belonged to me.

Every day Leif would come directly after his football practice with the food I'd requested smuggled inside his leather jacket. We would work on his homework, and then watch television and eat the food he brought. Being with Leif made me smile. I loved every moment we spent together. However, at night when the soul sat in my room and played for me, music seemed to fill the lonely places. I had a need for the soul I didn't understand. My desire for him scared, and fascinated me. My last night in the hospital his voice joined the strum of the guitar. He put words to my lullaby.

*"The life I walk binds my hands*
*it makes me take things that I don't understand*
*I walk this dark world unknowing of what they hold true,*
*forgetting the me I once knew,*
*until you.*
*The life I walk eternally was all I knew*
*nothing more held me here to this earth*
*until you.*
*I feel the pain of every heart I take*
*I feel the desire to replace all that I have grown to hate*
*Darkness holds me close but the light still draws my empty soul*
*The emptiness where I used pain to fill the hole*
*no longer controls me, no longer calls me*
*because of you."*

As my eyelids grew heavy and sleep crept over me, my heart ached for the pain in his words. They were words I knew meant more to him than I understood. The song he'd filled my nights with was much deeper than anything I'd ever known.

Miranda ran up to me the moment Leif opened the front door of the school and held it for me as I walked inside. The excitement on her face caused her brown eyes to twinkle. I smiled, waiting on her to explain the cause for her joyous behavior on a Monday morning. My being back at school couldn't be the reason for the euphoria on her face. Since I'd come home from the hospital she'd spent a good deal of time with me. My returning to school wouldn't cause this response.

She stopped and glanced up at Leif. He cleared his throat. "Um, I'll see you in a few minutes," he excused himself with a smile and headed toward my locker carrying my books.

"Okay, he's gone. Now, tell me what has you in such good spirits this morning."

She linked her arm in mine and leaned close to my ear. "Dank Walker is here. Like, at our school. Like, as in, enrolled at our school. Can you believe it? I mean, I know he went to a high school in Mobile, Alabama up until last year when his band landed a hit song and started playing all over the United States instead of just the Southeast. GAH! Can you believe he is here! At our school? I guess if he had to go back to high school, our little quaint coastal town is preferable to somewhere in Alabama. But still, I can't believe this."

I couldn't help but smile at Miranda's excitement even if I didn't have a clue who Dank Walker was. I'd never heard of him or his band before. I followed Miranda's giddy expression when my eyes found the soul. Last night I'd fought sleep to see if he would appear in my bedroom and sing me to sleep. He hadn't come. Seeing him now made me want to sigh in relief. The thought that I might not see him again had scared me. I smiled at him knowing I should act as if he wasn't there but I couldn't. Somewhere along the way, I'd come to rely on his presence. His dark blue eyes were pleased and less haunted than I remembered. I wanted to walk up to him and say something but I couldn't in this hall full of people. He nodded as if answering a question but his eyes never left mine. A tight smile formed on his face to replace the pleased smile I'd received. Then, as if in slow motion, he turned his attention to the blond girl who stood giggling and holding up a magazine and a pen for him to take.

I watched as if lost in a strange dream as he smiled and nodded at the girl's words. He signed the magazine she thrust into his hands and handed it back to her. I heard Miranda saying something beside me but it sounded as if she were miles away. Something was wrong. I took a step toward him unable to look away. He smiled at me with his sexy, crooked grin that produced his one perfect dimple. Suddenly his smile seemed apologetic as he once again turned from me to take something from the hands of another girl and signed it. I froze, trying to process what my eyes were seeing.

"Okay, Pagan, you're really going to have to snap out of it. Leif is coming and if he sees you looking at Dank Walker like you want to gobble him up there is going to be a problem."

I tore my eyes from the soul and stared over at my friend. "What?" I managed to ask through the questions swarming in my head.

Miranda grinned and shook her head. "Jeez, girl, you're worse than me. At least I didn't go that whack when I saw him in the office earlier. Of course, he didn't seem real bothered by your reaction either. Which is a good thing, considering you seem a might bit stalkerish."

I shook my head not understanding. "What?" I asked again.

"I've figured out the big news," Leif said from behind me, and I knew I should turn and look at him but I couldn't just yet. Everyone could see the soul. Nothing made sense. I closed my eyes and took a deep breath and then opened them to see Miranda watching me with an amused expression on her face.

"You see him?" I asked in a whisper. Her gaze flickered cautiously behind me to where I knew Leif stood and then they darted over to where the soul stood.

Once her eyes came back to mine she nodded slowly. "Um, yes, but what 'him' are we talking about?" she asked in a hushed whisper. I glanced quickly over to where the soul was still talking to students and signing things. Miranda leaned close to my ear. "That is Dank Walker, everyone sees him. Did you take some serious pain meds this morning? Because you're acting strange."

Dank Walker. The soul, *my* soul, was Dank Walker the rocker? A hand rested on my shoulder and I turned slowly around to face Leif. His concerned frown was identical to Miranda's. I shook my head to clear it and forced a smile. "Mom made me take some of my pain pills this morning and I think they're messing with my head," I lied, grasping at the excuse Miranda had just given me. Leif smiled and slipped his arm protectively around my shoulders.

"Ah, well, I'll take care of you. Come on, let's get you to your first class. I've already got your books." I walked beside Leif, relieved, yet disappointed we wouldn't be walking past the soul. I kept waiting to see if I would wake up from this strange dream and hear the soul playing softly in my room.

I arrived at English Literature before I realized Leif had been guiding me to it. He turned me around to face him. "If you need me, text me and I will be here in a second, okay?" I nodded and he gave me a quick kiss before turning and leaving me at the door of my classroom. I walked inside, fighting the urge to glance back and see the crowd of people around the soul, whom they called Dank Walker. I sat down at the first desk I came to and started to open my book when a warm tingling ran through my body. Startled, I glanced up. Dank was making his way toward me. I chanced a peek over at the other kids in the class. Everyone's eyes were on him. Girls were giggling and whispering. This had to be some sort of insane dream. He took the seat behind me and I fought the urge to shiver at the warming sensation his nearness seemed to be causing. This hadn't happened before.

"I don't believe we've met. I'm Dank Walker." His familiar, smooth drawl sure didn't sound like I was dreaming.

I turned around to look at him. If I'd taken pain pills this morning I would be convinced I was tripping. There was no excuse for this hallucination. "I don't understand," I said simply.

An apologetic smile tugged at his full lips. Were his lips fuller now that he was flesh and blood?

"I know, and I'm sorry."

Was it too much to ask for him to elaborate? If this was real then it would be awfully nice if he could explain to me how all of a sudden he could be seen by the rest of the living world. Better yet, why did they all believe him to be a rock star? He didn't say anything else but his eyes never left mine. Someone walked by and asked him for an autograph and he shook his head without taking his eyes off me. Everyone in the room seemed to be watching us. Talking to him here wouldn't get me any answers. I tore my eyes from his warm gaze and turned back around in my seat. If I didn't wake up soon then I'd worry about a better explanation than 'I'm sorry'.

"Settle down, settle down." Mr. Brown's voice carried over the excited whispering and occasional giggles. "It's very exciting, I realize, to have a," Mr. Brown waved a hand in Dank's direction, "young man among us, whose talents many of you enjoy. However, this is a time to learn the beauty that English Literature holds for us. We can moon and swoon over Mr. Walker during our lunchtime.

"Now, today we're going to move on from our study of Shakespeare. We have briefly touched upon him this year because this was not your first exposure to Shakespeare and I feel it is important to focus on some other famous playwrights. The ancient Greek playwright, Aeschylus, was just as influential in his works. In fact, various ancient sources attribute between seventy and ninety plays to him. I believe on Friday I asked you all to read the chapter in your book concerning Aeschylus, and since it was the weekend I know this was a huge request. However, can anyone in here tell me something you learned from your reading?" Mr. Brown clasped his hands together across his chest to rest just above his round stomach. The room remained quiet. I'd spent my weekend trying to catch up on all my missed schoolwork and reading about Aeschylus hadn't been very important. Besides, focusing right now would be difficult.

"Only six of his tragedies have survived intact: *The Persians, Seven against Thebes, The Suppliants*, and the trilogy known as *The Oresteia*, consisting of the three tragedies *Agamemnon, The Libation Bearers* and *The Eumenides*." Dank's smooth voice carried over the room and Mr. Brown stared back at him surprised.

"Seven, Mr. Walker. You forgot *Prometheus Bound*."

"*Prometheus Bound*'s authorship is disputed. It's widely thought to be the work of a later author." Dank's voice held a tone of boredom.

Mr. Brown straightened his short, wide frame and stared down at Dank with a slow smile coming over his face. "Why, yes it is, but that information was not within your textbook." He looked at the rest of the class grinning like someone had brought him a dozen doughnuts. "It appears that our musical friend is well educated."

I heard a quiet chuckle from behind me and I glanced over my shoulder to see Dank's eyes on me. Did he read minds? Did he have super powers? I turned away from him and closed my eyes, trying to get the questions lodging themselves in my head about Dank Walker pushed aside long enough to pay attention in class.

"Very good, very good indeed. Now, as stated on your syllabus for the year, you're all to have purchased copies of *The Oresteia: Agamemnon; The Libation Bearers; The Eumenides*. We are going to begin our study on Aeschylus by reading his work, *Agamemnon*. Who brought their book to class as requested on Friday?" I stared down at my textbook and notebook. Leif hadn't known to get the paperback from my locker. "Ah, and our new student surprises me yet again." I glanced up to see Mr. Brown nodding toward Dank's desk. "That is the book on your desk is it not Mr. Walker?"

"Yes sir," Dank answered and I involuntarily shivered. I thought I heard another soft chuckle come from behind me.

"Well, then would you please begin reading for me? Since it appears that the rest of the students in this room, who were in fact here on Friday, seem to be suffering from memory loss."

Dank cleared his throat and began reading. "Dear gods, set me free from all the pain, the long watch I keep, one whole year awake... propped on my arms, crouched on the roofs of Atreus like a dog. I know the stars by heart, the armies of the night, and there in the lead the ones that bring us snow or the crops of summer, bring us all we have - our great kings of the sky, I know them, when they rise and when they fall...and now I watch for the light, the signal-fire breaking out of Troy, shouting Troy is taken. So, she commands, full of her high hopes."

The class went by so quickly with Dank's hypnotic voice commanding the room. The ring of the bell caused me to jump. I shook my head trying to get out of the trance his reading had put me in. I stood up and reached for my books, knowing Leif would be at the door waiting for me, ready to take my books to my next class. It took supreme effort not to glance back at Dank.

The sound of giggling girls and fawning fans allowed me to reach Leif without breaking down and turning to sneak a glance at Dank.

"Fun class?" Leif raised his eyebrows and nodded his head toward where I knew Dank stood surrounded by female admirers.

I shrugged. "Not really. Tragic Greek plays, you know, the usual." Leif shot me one of his easy grins before reaching for my books.

"Glad I made my move before Dank Walker showed up," Leif said in a joking voice that sounded forced.

I didn't look up at him. "What do you mean?" Did he notice the pink flush on my cheeks when he said Dank's name? God I hoped not.

"The dude can't seem to take his eyes off you. Not that I can blame him." Leif slipped his arm around my shoulders and pulled me close as if he needed to hold onto me. Instant guilt swamped me. The way I shivered and melted when near Dank wasn't fair to Leif. A strange pull inside me to turn around caused me to grab Leif's arm for support. Maybe this was a dream after all. It was almost as if some iron-like hold was trying to force me to stop and turn back.

"Are you okay?" Leif's voice was edged with concern. I knew he was thinking I'd lost my mind. Nothing about the way I was acting was sane.

I smiled up at him reassuringly. "I'm good." Unable to fight the invisible tug, I glanced back and my eyes immediately found Dank surrounded by girls, but his eyes were on me. Even from this distance I could feel the warmth of his intense gaze.

"He seems to be a hot item," Leif mumbled as his gaze followed mine. I jerked my head back around, furious with myself for giving in and searching him out. The concern in Leif's voice said it all. I needed to get a grip.

"I don't really do the whole rocker thing. I honestly haven't even got a clue what he sings or what band he's in."

Leif kissed the top of my head. "I wish the rock star had heard that." He seemed to relax beside me.

*"That's not true, Pagan. You enjoy your own little private concert each night while you sleep."*

I froze gripping Leif's arm tighter. What the heck was that? Had Dank just talked in my head? God this had to be a dream! It was getting crazier by the minute. I let go of Leif's arm and pinched myself as hard as I possibly could.

"What are you doing?" Leif asked with a look of confusion on his face. My face grew warm. Within seconds I would be bright red. I wasn't sure if it was from the fact Dank had just somehow spoken in my ear yet he was an entire hallway length away from me or the fact I was pinching myself in the hallway like a nut case.

"Relax, Pagan, no one hears me but you. Wipe the lovely blush from your face. Your friend, who seems to think you belong to him, is going to think you're crazy."

I turned around, this time needing to see where he was. It was Dank's voice I heard. Just as clearly as if he were standing right beside me leaning toward my ear. Dank wasn't right beside me. He was where I had remembered: standing on the opposite end of the hallway, listening to a red-headed freshman girl who seemed to be on cloud nine to have the rock star's attention. His eyes left hers and found mine. He winked and gave me his wicked smile before staring back down at the girl at his side. I swallowed the fear running through me and turned away from him. Had he actually just spoken to me from across the hallway and no one heard him?

"Are you okay, Pagan?" Leif's voice broke into my moment of panic and I managed to force a smile and nod.

"Yes, I just thought I forgot something, but I didn't."

Leif chuckled. "The medication still messing with you?" he asked in a voice that helped bring me back to normalcy. He was normal. He was real.

"Um, yes, I think it is." If only I'd taken pain medicine this morning, like I kept claiming, then I could blame all this on chemicals. But I knew the truth. I hadn't taken anything. I was going crazy all on my own.

"I talked to Leif during Speech and I suggested the four of us go see a movie tonight to celebrate your return to school," Miranda said from across the cafeteria table. I'd been so lost in my thoughts I hadn't realized she'd sat down across from me.

I glanced up. "That sounds like a great idea."

Miranda frowned, tilted her head, and leaned closer to me. "Are you okay?"

I forced a smile and nodded. Convincing my best friend I wasn't internally freaking out was going to be difficult. As expected, she raised her eyebrows and gave me the 'I don't believe you' eye as she sat back. Luckily, Wyatt chose that moment to join us so she wouldn't get a chance to probe me further.

"Tonight after Leif gets done with football practice, we're all going to the movies to celebrate Pagan's recovery."

Wyatt glanced over at me with a concerned face. "You up for that?"

I nodded. "Sure, I feel much better. I need to get away and do something normal."

Miranda's smile returned. "Then it's settled. Now, all that is left is to decide what movie we're going to see." Miranda's eyes stared at something over my head. "Ugh, figures." She said in a tone of disgust.

I glanced back to see what she found so irritating. Kendra walked in with her arm tucked inside Dank's elbow, smiling coyly up at him while he talked to her. He obviously enjoyed her attention. He wouldn't be the first male to fall victim to her attentions. Kendra made a complete package of perfect, if you left out her personality. I turned my head back around, hoping I could cover up the churning emotions in my stomach. The sight of her on his arm made me a little sick.

"It would be Kendra that got the rock star," Miranda said in a disgusted tone before taking a bite of her salad.

"I hope I'm not hearing jealousy in your voice. Considering that would be a blow to my ego," Wyatt said teasingly and Miranda glared up at him.

"Of course not. I just wish Dank Walker hadn't decided to give his attention to that skanky bitch. There are plenty of other beautiful girls in this school who would be much better choices."

Wyatt chuckled. "Like who?"

Miranda shrugged. "I don't know. Just someone who isn't Kendra." Wyatt laughed out loud and shook his head.

"What did I miss?" Leif asked as he sat down beside me.

"Nothing," I responded a little too quickly.

Wyatt nodded toward where Dank and Kendra sat at a table alone. "It appears Miranda thinks anyone would have been a better choice for the rock star than Kendra."

Leif nodded. "She's probably right. But as long as he has stopped ogling my girl, I don't care who he gives his attention to."

Miranda raised her eyebrows at me in surprise. "Really, he's been ogling you?"

I rolled my eyes. "No." My quick response didn't even sound believable to my own ears.

"Yes, he has," Leif said, reaching for my hand under the table. He gave me a gentle squeeze as if to reassure me. I sighed and relaxed. No point arguing with him. I knew Dank watched me more often than anyone else. I hadn't realized how possessive I felt toward him until I'd seen Kendra getting his attention. He could go sing Kendra to sleep with his guitar and hauntingly beautiful music. I heard a low chuckle and turned to look at both Leif and Wyatt whose mouths were full of food. I froze and glanced back at the table where Dank sat in a private conversation with Kendra. His eyes left hers and gave me an amused glance before turning back to the perfect blond beside him.

# Chapter Six

"I do believe this is your first football game," my mother said, grinning from the kitchen sink where she stood draining bow tie noodles.

I shrugged. "I guess."

She glanced up at me. "And you're going out with the quarterback when it's over?" I started to answer her when a soul walked into the kitchen through the closed patio doors. I stiffened. It'd been a long time since a soul had wandered through our house. The soul appeared young. Her hair hung down her back in long, curly blond locks. It seemed to float around her waist. I started to do the standard and act like I didn't see her, but she stopped directly in front of me and began studying me. Her eyes seemed translucent and her eyelashes were incredibly long but so blond they were almost undetectable. Her head tilted to one side as she walked closer to me, watching me as if I were some sort of science experiment that befuddled her.

"Honey?" My mom's voice woke me up out of the trance. I jerked my gaze away from the soul, which proved hard because she stood so close to me that I could reach out and touch her.

"Um, yes, sorry." Mom no longer seemed amused.

She frowned at me with the colander of noodles held forgotten in her hands. "Are you okay, Pagan? Maybe you should stay home and rest. A whole week of school had to have been difficult after what you've been through." I forced myself not to shiver when a cold hand touched my hair.

"It's pretty." The musical sound of the soul's voice startled me. I jerked back from her.

"Pagan?" I took a deep, calming breath and forced a smile I hoped was normal.

"I'm fine, just a little nervous. I need to finish getting ready before Miranda and Wyatt get here."

Mom nodded and her smile returned. "Alright, then. I guess nerves are understandable when one is going on a date with such a hottie." She winked and I held my fake smile before turning and fleeing the room. I closed my bedroom door and turned to watch and see if the soul followed me.

"Are you looking for me?" The musical voice came from behind me. I swung around in surprise and let out a startled yelp.

"What are you doing?" I asked, confused. Why had souls proceeded to start talking to me? She giggled and it sounded similar to a chime of bells.

"It is appointed," she said simply and walked closer to me. I held out both hands as if it would hold her off.

"Don't come any closer," I said, realizing for the first time in my life I was completely terrified of a soul.

She frowned. "You're not very friendly."

I let out a short laugh, "What? I'm not friendly to a ghost who floats into my house and starts touching me? Well, excuse my rudeness but this is a little disturbing."

Her frown seemed to take on an understanding expression. "Ah, yes. Well, I guess I just assumed you were used to us."

So she knew I could see souls. "Who are you?" I asked again, wishing my voice at least sounded steady instead of unmistakably trembling. She didn't answer, but went back to studying me silently. "I need to get ready to go before my friends get here. If you have no purpose for being here then could you just go find another house to wander through?"

Her tinkling laughter filled my room again. "I do not wander through the homes of people," she said as if I'd just said the silliest thing she'd ever heard. "It is appointed," she said again, smiling brightly.

I started to ask her what she was referring to when, once again, I stood alone in my room. I turned around in a circle, expecting to see her drifting around but she was gone. Needing to hear the normalcy of my mother's off-key singing while she cooked dinner, I went and opened the door to my bedroom. I needed to see Dank. I wanted answers. Before Dank, souls didn't talk to me. I had liked it that way. I would like to keep it that way. I did not like the idea of souls walking up to me and touching me and talking to me. I could deal with their presence but I preferred to ignore them and in return get treated like everyone else. I made one more quick sweep of my room and closed my door quietly. Putting some distance between me and the door, I walked to the other side of the room. The last thing I needed was for my mom to hear what I was about to do.

"Dank," I said aloud. He had talked to me from across a crowded hallway. I figured he could hear me anywhere. But then I wasn't the expert on soul beckoning. I'd never felt the need to beckon one before. I waited but nothing happened. I turned around to check behind me. "Dank?" I said again, feeling stupid. The room remained empty. With a defeated sigh I went back to my bedroom door and opened it again. I needed to stop playing with the supernatural and get ready.


"GOOO PIRATES!" Miranda cheered loudly from her seat beside me. We were up by two touchdowns and the crowd began cheering wildly. Only four minutes left in the game and I hadn't seen Dank anywhere. Apparently, Kendra hadn't seen him either because I'd watched her on the football field cheering. She kept scanning the crowd for him. Her reasons for wanting to see him were completely different from mine of course. Not to mention the fact that hers were not nearly as important. With every scowl on her face, I knew she didn't see the elusive Dank Walker. I needed to find him before the game ended. Going out with Leif afterward to celebrate the victory would be hindered by the unanswered questions in my head.

"Would you stop scanning the crowd for the rock star and watch your boyfriend," Miranda hissed in my ear. I should have known she would figure me out.

I frowned. "I'm not looking for the rock star. Football just bores me."

Miranda laughed and rolled her eyes. "You would date the mouthwatering quarterback and then admit you're bored by football."

I shrugged and then turned my attention back to the action on the field. The moment my eyes landed on Kendra, I saw her face light up as she zoned in on someone toward the bottom of the stands. I couldn't see him from where I sat but I knew he'd arrived. That would be the only reason Kendra would have exchanged her annoyed expression for one of utter delight. I glanced over at Miranda and Wyatt who both were watching the game. Kendra's expression wasn't something they were paying attention to.

I reached for my purse. "I'm going to go get a drink, do you want one?" I asked hoping they said no. I didn't want to be rushed. I needed to get Dank alone and get some answers.

Miranda stared up at me as I stood and shook her head. "No, the game is almost over and we're going to the Grill to celebrate. We can get drinks there."

I slipped my purse on my shoulder. "I'm thirsty now. I'll meet you on the field when this is over." Miranda peeked around me and out into the crowd. I didn't have to ask to know she was searching for Dank. Luckily he hadn't walked into view.

Miranda glanced back at me and shrugged. "Okay." I turned and walked away quickly before she spotted Dank or decided she wanted something from the concession stand.

Dank stood with his arms crossed, as if he were bored, watching the game on the field. His eyes found mine the moment I came around the corner. A small smile touched his lips. I didn't have time to deal with his smart comments about my coming to find him.

"I need to talk to you alone, now," I said in a whisper as I walked past him and into the dark parking lot. I didn't turn around to see if he was following me. I could feel his presence. Once I knew we were out of sight of everyone else, I turned around and faced him. "Who is she?" I demanded.

Dank frowned. "Be more specific, please."

I sighed and closed my eyes against the distraction his eyes always presented. Seeing him in the moonlight made it hard for me to concentrate. "The soul who came into my house and touched me and talked to me. She said 'it is appointed' to me twice."

Dank visibly tensed and stepped closer to me. "What?" he asked with a look of surprise on his face.

"A soul came into my house. She touched me and talked to me. Souls never talked to me, before you. She even came into my bedroom," I said in a whisper, afraid someone might overhear me.

"She said 'it is appointed'?" he asked with a tight edge to his voice. I could tell he was trying to control his temper, I just didn't know why he was angry. I nodded, watching him closely.

He stalked farther into the darkness and then turned his angry glare up to the sky. "Don't fuck with me," he said loudly in a cold, hard voice. I backed away, not sure what he was yelling at. He stood with his back to me taking deep breaths and I waited, wishing I hadn't brought him out here into the darkness alone.

He turned slowly around. Even in the darkness I could clearly see his blue eyes. They reminded me of bright sapphires reflecting rays of the sun. "I'm going to be watching." His voice sounded much deeper than before. I took a step backwards, terrified by the startling glow in his eyes and the growl I could hear coming from deep within his chest.

"If she comes near you or any other...soul, comes near you and talks to you again, then you warn them that you're going to tell me. Do you understand?" I was scared. Not of Dank but of...something.

"Who is she?" I asked again.

A tortured look came over his face before he turned away from me. "Someone who has come to right a wrong."

I stepped closer to him, needing to know more, but he shook his head in protest and then he was gone. I stood alone in the dark parking lot. In light of current events I didn't like being out here alone. Even if I knew Dank was close enough that he would come if I called him. Cheers erupted from the field, signaling that the game had ended. My questions were still unanswered. Frustrated with Dank and his determination to be evasive even though he seemed to be the cause of my screwed up life at the moment, I walked quickly back to the brightly-lit stadium. The field was full of celebrating pirates as I walked into the throngs of students and parents. I began searching for Miranda and Wyatt. A familiar chuckle caught my attention and I turned to see Kendra with her hands on Dank's chest as he stared down at her with a smile on his face. I froze.

He seemed carefree and pleased by the attention of the blond cheerleader, when moments ago he'd been cursing at the sky and telling me to threaten any more talking souls I came in contact with. The urge to walk over to Kendra and jerk her by the hair until she was a good ten feet away from Dank was hard to resist. His eyes lifted from Kendra's and found me. He nodded as if to say hello before gazing back down at the girl in his arms. I swallowed the feeling of betrayal and tore my eyes off the two of them. Dank didn't belong to me so he wasn't actually betraying me. That reminder didn't make me feel better. At times it seemed as if Dank Walker and the soul were two completely different beings. The soul I trusted. Dank Walker confused me.

"Pagan!" Miranda's voice cut through the celebrating voices. I turned around, not sure I could face her right now. I glanced back at the parking lot, thinking of a way I could escape. But home didn't seem safe anymore. The beautiful blond soul scared me. "Pagan?" Miranda called again and I turned my attention back to the crowd, knowing I should go to her. Leif would be expecting me. However, the me he would be getting wasn't the one he deserved. I wasn't cheering about the victory. Instead, I was terrified of the unknown.

"*Go to them. I'm here. You're safe.*" Dank's voice came through loud and clear over the excited voices of the crowd. Just as before, no one else seemed to hear him. I searched the faces around me for his familiar one.

"Jeez, Pagan, are you deaf! Where've you been? Come on." Miranda grabbed my arm and began pulling me back through the victorious crowd. I let her pull me and forced myself to smile. Leif would expect me to. Miranda and Wyatt would expect me to. I was going to end up being diagnosed as mental if I didn't get a grip on myself.

"There he is!" Miranda yelled back at me as she pulled me toward Leif. He'd just emerged from the field house, freshly changed into a pair of faded jeans and a clean jersey. I took a deep breath and put a smile on my face. He glanced our way and I waved at him. A huge grin broke out on his face and he ran toward me. Before I knew it he was pulling me up against his chest. I didn't have time to prepare myself for his lips covering mine. His arms around me were gentle because of my still healing ribs. He reminded me of warmth and safety. I ran my hands up his chest, hoping to hold onto him a little while longer and pretend I really was safe. His hands slipped into my hair and tilted my head back as he took the kiss deeper. I drank him in. I needed this sense of normalcy. This false sense of security. Leif was real and represented all things secure. I needed that connection to the world. I needed what he offered right now. However, dancing dangerously in the back of my mind, were thoughts of another mouth, which seemed to stir things much wilder inside of me. A craving that represented all the things I feared. I closed my eyes tighter, trying to fight off the desire to have Dank's arms pulling me close, his perfectly sculpted lips against mine. This was safe. Leif was healthy for me.

He broke the kiss and pulled back only a little and his breathing, I realized, was ragged, unlike mine. He appeared dazed. "That was even better than I'd imagined," he said breathlessly. The familiar twinge of guilt I'd been dealing with since Dank had gotten under my skin reminded me this was the right choice.

"Okay, you two either need to get a freakin' room or come up for air so we can go get some food. I'm starving." Wyatt's teasing voice broke into the little world we'd been lost in among the throngs of people.

Leif winked at me and slipped his arm around my shoulder. "Let's eat," he said, grinning like a little boy who'd just been given candy. I'd clung to him because of what he represented in my life not because I desired him, but I pushed it out of my mind. Thinking about it just made the guilt worse.

"After tonight's game I don't see how the scouts can keep away," Wyatt said, grinning across the booth from Leif and me.

Leif chuckled. "One game won't bring down the college scouts, you know that."

Wyatt lifted a French fry to his mouth. "A couple more like that one and they will descend," he said, sure of himself. Leif's thumb rubbed my hand. He'd started holding my hand whenever we were together. It was sweet.

"Oh, gag, did they have to come here? I mean, really, why doesn't he just take octopus-girl to a hotel and let us eat in peace?" Miranda said in an annoyed voice as she flashed a knowing look my way. I glanced over to see Dank walk in the door with a very clingy Kendra at his side. I reached for my soda and decided to study the business cards placed under the Plexiglas on top of the table.

"I think the only way she can get any closer to him is if she wraps her legs around him and he is forced to carry her." Miranda said in a disgusted tone.

Wyatt chuckled. "Alright, Miranda, leave the poor girl alone. It looks like the rock star has his hands full with keeping her from mauling him. He doesn't need you making snide comments." Miranda giggled and leaned over and laid her head on Wyatt's shoulder.

"Mauling? I like that one. Wish I'd thought of it." Wyatt shook his head as he crammed another fry into his grinning mouth.

Leif sighed. "She has issues that make her act like she does." I stared up at him and realized he seemed concerned rather than amused.

Miranda rolled her eyes. "You would know. You dated her for like three years."

Leif gazed down at me. "Yes, I did, but only because the one girl I wanted seemed to dislike me so completely."

I smiled and squeezed his hand. "I was stupid." It was true. Getting to know Leif had taught me that judging others wasn't only wrong but it caused you to miss out on friendships with special people.

His eyes got serious and he leaned down and stopped right before his lips touched mine. "You're brilliant. Maybe a little slow on the uptake, but brilliant nonetheless." His lips touched mine gently. Again, I felt safe. A deep growl startled me and I pulled back, staring up at Leif to see if he'd been growling. The confused frown on his face told me it hadn't been him. His thumb brushed across my bottom lip and the growling started up again. It definitely wasn't Leif making the animal noises. "You okay?" he asked softly.

"Sorry, I thought you said something." I explained, forcing a smile. He grinned and dropped his hand from my face. The growling subsided and I glanced around the room. Dank sat in a corner booth beside Kendra, who appeared to be talking excitedly to another cheerleader beside them. His dark eyes watched me with a possessive gleam. It'd been him. He'd growled. How was he doing that? I could feel Miranda watching me and I didn't want her asking me any more questions. I turned back to my food and forced a French fry into my mouth. Leif and Wyatt had resumed talking about the game, so I had time to get my focus back on my friends and off Dank. Leif leaned back against the booth and released my hand, slipping his behind my shoulders and then gently pulled me against him.

Miranda smiled. "So, when are we going to go pick out our dresses for the Homecoming Dance?" she asked me. I frowned at her. Leif and I hadn't talked about the Homecoming Dance. We were dating exclusively but he hadn't said anything about taking me to the dance. I'd already decided to stay home and watch old movies and eat popcorn that night. Miranda flicked her eyes from me to Leif a few times as if assessing the situation.

"You've asked her right?" she asked with an annoyed tone. Leif turned his head and gazed down at me.

"I just assumed that it was understood. Was I supposed to ask?" The concerned frown on his face was adorable. I smiled up at him, hoping to reassure him. I didn't like to upset him. He seemed so emotionally tender.

"Leif, you're always supposed to ask a girl to a dance. Assuming is a bad thing." Miranda's corrective tone made me laugh. Leif's frown eased and he slid his finger under my chin and gently caressed my jaw line with the pad of his thumb.

"Pagan, will you do me the honor of being my date for the

Homecoming Dance? The prospect of not being able to hold you in my arms all night is heartbreaking."

Miranda sighed from across the table. "Okay, that was beautiful. Why didn't you ask me like that?" She asked Wyatt.

Wyatt shot Leif an annoyed frown. "Thanks, buddy. Next time you decide to break out your romantic side, could you do it alone?"

I laughed and Leif continued gazing down at me. I nodded and he leaned down to kiss me. I mentally prepared myself for the growl and the moment I heard it, low and angry in my ears, I smiled.

# Chapter Seven

The moment I tried to open the front door and found it locked, I knew I was in trouble. The note on the bar from my mother telling me she and Roger had gone out to a late movie sent a shiver of fear through me. I didn't want to be home alone. I hadn't asked Miranda to come stay the night with me because I'd planned on sleeping in bed with my mom tonight. I walked into my bedroom and scanned every inch of it for long blond hair. No sign of the freaky soul. I glanced back at the bathroom and thought of the shower I really wanted. Going in there and turning on the shower and closing the curtain scared me. I kept getting visions of horror movies I'd seen, where bad things happened when someone took a shower. I'd never be able to take a shower without Mom home. Maybe not even then. Oh crap! I was going to become the incredible stinking girl! If I tried to convince my mom to come into the bathroom with me so I could shower she'd think I'd lost it. I plopped down on my bed and let out a defeated sigh.

"What's wrong?" a voice asked from my doorway. I shot straight up screaming. However, it died almost immediately when I saw Dank leaning against the door frame watching me.

"Dank." I took a deep breath to calm my racing heart.

"Sorry, I didn't realize you were so wound up about this," he said, frowning and walking into the room. I sat back down on my bed and let out a shallow laugh.

"Well excuse me if strange souls showing up in my house, talking to me and touching me freak me out a little." I shot him an accusatory look. "Then, I ask you about it and you curse into the darkness and get all angry."

He walked over and sat down at the end of my bed. "I'm sorry about that. I shouldn't have scared you that way." There was no mistaking the concerned tone of his voice.

"Well, can you tell me what is happening, who she is?" I asked. He shook his head and immediately turned his gaze away from me.

"No, that's the only thing I can't do for you. Ask me anything else in the world, Pagan, and I'll make sure it's yours but that I cannot do." his voice sounded intense and pained at the same time. It disappointed me but I knew pushing the subject was pointless.

"Why are you here, then?" I asked remembering how less than

an hour ago I'd left him in a corner booth with Kendra curled up against his side. He stood up and walked over to the window and stared outside.

"Until I know everything is fine...until I take care of what must be done, I'll be spending the nights here in your room." He turned back to me with a determined expression. "I have to protect you." He motioned toward the door. "If you want to take that shower, I'll make sure you're completely safe while you do so."

Heck yes, I wanted that shower. I started to get up and then sat back down, glaring at him. "Can you read my mind?" This wasn't the first time he'd known what I was thinking.

He grinned wickedly at me. "Not exactly. It's more like I can feel your fears so strongly I can hear them." I nodded and thought of the time he'd chuckled where only I could hear him, as if he'd heard me in the cafeteria thinking about him and Kendra.

I stared back at him. "You heard me in the cafeteria when you were with Kendra, I wasn't scared then."

He raised his eyebrows slightly. "You weren't?" My face grew warm and I turned and left the room before he could see me blush.

I started to close the bathroom door when I turned and looked at the walls knowing a soul could come in at any time. I stared back down the hall where Dank lay lounging on my bed. He couldn't see the soul if she came into the bathroom. His head turned immediately toward me. A slow wicked smile formed on his mouth.

"I would love to accompany you into the bathroom while you shower and if I were truly as wicked as you think I am, I would do just that. However, I can feel any soul intent on entering this house before they even come inside. I would be there before any other entered. You're safe with me right here," he finished with a wink. I closed the door quickly before he said anything else to embarrass me.


I slipped on a pair of cut-off sweat pants and a tank top instead of my usual night gown. If I was going to have company while I slept, I needed to wear clothes. My heart raced at the thought of Dank being in my bedroom, on my bed and I took several deep breaths to calm my thoughts and emotions.

"Pagan, honey, are you in the bathroom?" Mom called from the hallway. I opened the door and glanced past her to the bed where

Dank still lay lounging.

"She can't see or hear me. Calm down."

I looked back to my mother, who stood, smiling in the doorway. "Did you have a good time with Leif?"

"Yes, we won the game and went out with Miranda and Wyatt afterwards to the Grill. It was nice." I said thinking of his kissing me and once again my mind went back to the incredibly sexy nonhuman male in my room, who I couldn't seem to keep out of my head.

Mom laughed. "Nice, huh? Poor kid, he hasn't got a clue you're one hard nut to crack. Ah, well, that's good for now. One day, the right guy will come along and you'll be so swept away, you won't be able to see straight. Enjoy the others until then." She kissed my cheek and headed toward her room.

As I stepped into my room, I stared down at what appeared to be a sleeping Dank. I closed my bedroom door softly, not wanting to wake him. He opened his eyes and stared up at me, smiling.

"There is no chance you would let me sleep on the bed too?"

I shook my head and laughed. "No, there isn't."

He sighed and sat up, "I'd already guessed as much but I was hoping for a moment of pity from the 'hard nut'."

I frowned, hating that he'd heard my mother. I really didn't want Dank to know I wasn't completely in love with Leif. It was better that way. I went to my closet in search of the sleeping bag I'd bought to go camping last summer.

"I don't sleep Pagan, I was teasing you."

I turned around and frowned. "Okay, I guess that makes sense... for normal souls. They don't have bodies but you do, then you don't. It's like you can just choose if you want to be human or soul. That isn't normal, is it?" I asked, not sure exactly how any of this worked. The one thing I knew was that it did not work the way I'd always been taught. Sunday School had it all wrong.

He chuckled and sat down on the love seat beside my window. "I'm not a soul, per se. That's all you can know." He reached for the guitar I hadn't noticed standing in the corner behind the chair.

"Go to sleep, Pagan. You're safe and you need rest." He began strumming on the guitar and I turned to my bed and pulled back the covers before slipping inside. The lights went out and I glanced over at Dank.

"No need to sleep with the lights on. I can see either way," he explained. I nodded and forced myself to close my eyes. I wanted to ask more questions but I knew he wasn't going to answer them tonight. The sound of the music began to soothe me. Dank's low voice joined the guitar and I got lost in the sound and the safety of his presence...

"You weren't meant for the ice, you weren't made for the pain.

The world that lives inside of me was not the world you were meant to contain.

You were meant for castles and living in the sun. The cold running through me should have made you run.

Yet you stay. Holding onto me, yet you stay, reaching out a hand that I push away. The cold is not meant for you yet you stay, you stay, you stay. When I know it's not right for you.

The ice fills my veins and I can't feel the pain, yet you're there like the heat that sends me screaming in fear.

I can't feel the warmth I need to feel the ice. I want to hold it all in and numb it till I can't feel the knife.

Your heat threatens to melt it all and I know I can't bear the pain if the ice melts away.

So I push you away and I scream out your name and I know I can't need you yet you give anyway and I run wishing you would run too.

Yet you stay. Holding onto me yet you stay reaching out a hand that I push away. The cold is not meant for you yet you stay, you stay, you stay. When I know it's not right for you.

The blackness is my shield. I pull it closer still.

You're the light that I hide from, the light that I hate. You're the light to this darkness and I can't let you stay.

I need the dark around me like I need the ice in my veins.

The cold is my healer. The cold is my safe place. You aren't welcome with your heat you don't belong beside me.

I hate you yet I love, I don't want you yet I need you.

The dark will always be my cloak and you are the threat to unveil my pain, so leave. Leave and erase the memories.

I need to face the life that's meant for me. Don't stay and ruin all my plans.

You can't have my soul I'm not a man.

The empty vessel I dwell in is not meant to feel the heat you bring. I push you away and I push you away.

Yet you stay."

The sound of my mother's off-key singing and the smell of bacon woke me up. I stretched and squinted against the brightness of the late morning sun. Last night slowly came back to me and I sat up in bed and looked toward the now empty chair. I glanced around the room and realized I was alone. Had he left me? I'd trusted him to keep me safe. I got up, needing to open the door and be near my mother. Being alone wasn't on my 'to do' list. I turned back and noticed his guitar stood in the corner and a small amount of comfort returned, knowing a part of him was here. However, a guitar was not him, so I rushed downstairs.

"Well, good morning, Glory," my mother said from the stove. She put a piece of bacon on top of a paper towel-lined plate.

"Morning," I said in a voice raspy from the deep sleep I'd been in. The clearing of a male throat startled me and I turned to see Dank sitting on the couch watching me.

"You thought I left. I said I wouldn't," he said with a smile. I let out a sigh of relief and smiled weakly.

"Here, honey, go ahead and get you a pancake before they get cold and take some bacon. The coffee is fresh if you want some." She chuckled. "You look as if you need a pick me up."

I smiled and went to fix myself a plate. "It smells good," Dank said from his spot on the couch. I frowned, worrying about him not being able to eat.

He chuckled. "It's okay, Pagan, I don't need food. It's a perk." I poured a cup of coffee and spooned sugar and milk into it before heading to the table. "You look like you slept well," he said, taking in my appearance. I blushed thinking of my unbrushed hair, which I hadn't fixed due to the hasty escape from my empty bedroom. "Don't even think of brushing it. I like it, it's sexy." I rolled my eyes and sank down into the chair, and took a bite.

"So, what are your plans this morning, Sunshine?" Mom asked from the kitchen. I glanced over at her as she was fixing her plate.

"Um, I'm going shopping for a dress for the Homecoming Dance with Miranda, Wyatt, and Leif."

Dank chuckled. "So, Leif's wearing a dress?" I glared at him and then turned to my mom as she sat down at the table across from me.

"Oh, so Leif asked you to the dance? That's exciting. You can take the visa card with you. Just make sure you don't get anything red or yellow. Those colors aren't good with your complexion." I nodded and took another bite.

"Blue, soft blue," Dank said quietly as if he was thinking about it rather than saying it. I kept my eyes on my food.

"I have a date with the computer today. My newest manuscript is almost finished. I'm excited about this one more so than I have been about any others." Her voice had taken on the chipper tone it only had when she spoke of her writing.

"Or better yet, a really pale pink," Dank said and I stiffened. His words felt like a caress and it was taking all my strength to keep from shivering. He chuckled, and then stood up and walked toward the door. I wanted to ask him where he was going but I couldn't with my mom sitting here.



"Finally, we can go get food. I'm starving." Wyatt breathed a sigh of relief with Miranda's dress bag hanging over his shoulder.

"Whatever, it wasn't that bad. I mean we managed to find the perfect dresses in under four hours. I would say that was pretty impressive." Miranda smiled smugly.

Wyatt chuckled. "No, you took four hours. Pagan had hers picked out after one hour. Leif has already had time to take hers to the car and get himself a taco while we waited for you."

Leif held up both hands. "Leave me out of this one." He slipped an arm around my waist and bent down to kiss the top of my head. Being with him was just so easy.

"We're going to feed you, Wyatt, for all your hard work." I said teasingly and Miranda giggled.

"What was all his hard work? Sitting in a chair and saying, 'That's gorgeous get that one,' to every dress I tried on?"

I laughed and Wyatt shrugged. "What? I can't think you're beautiful no matter what you put on?"

Miranda smiled up at him and slid her arm around his waist. "I love you," she said without any hesitancy. I became a little uncomfortable in Leif's arms. I hoped he didn't get any ideas because those were not words I was ready to use in any form.

"I love you more," Wyatt replied, smiling back down at her.

"Get a room," Leif said jokingly and my tension eased. He seemed to always be able to do that for me. I watched as a soul walked around, studying people as if he were lost. That happened sometimes too. I always wondered if they were new souls, confused as to what had happened to them. It always made me sad. The soul looked over at me and I gave him a small smile but quickly turned away. I didn't want him coming up to me and speaking. I wasn't in the mood for talking souls at the moment.

"So, Pagan, where do you want to eat?" Leif asked and I glanced over at Wyatt who was mouthing, "Mexican" to me.

I smiled and turned back to Leif. "Tacos sound good."

Leif chuckled. "Are you sure, I can see and read lips, too, even though Wyatt seems to think I can't."

"No, really, I want Mexican. Salsa and chips sound good."

"Mexican it is."

We all turned and headed into the Mexican restaurant located inside the mall. The tingling sensation that someone was watching me caused me to glance back. The soul I'd noticed earlier had followed us and stood several feet away staring at me. I could tell by his lost expression he was a normal soul. The kind I'd dealt with all my life. I turned away as if I didn't see him. Ignoring him was for the best. That way he would continue on instead of wasting time with me. There was nothing I could do for him now.

*Please be in my room, please be in my room.* I chanted in my head as I walked upstairs past my mom's room where I heard her typing vigorously on her computer. I stepped inside and nearly sighed in relief at a very amused Dank lounging comfortably on my bed.

"I told you I would be here. Why do you doubt me?" I shrugged and thought about the fact he hadn't been with me all day.

"Did you really want me to tag along on your date?" he asked and I smiled and shook my head. "I didn't think so. Besides you were with friends and out in public. All was well. I was making sure of that." He spoke in a casual tone as if we weren't talking about supernatural beings. He nodded his head toward the dress hanging up in my closet, "Pale pink. I like it."

I blushed, thinking about the fact I'd only tried on pale pink dresses. The way I'd felt when he had suggested pale pink kept replaying through my mind and I couldn't think of any other color to try. I ducked my head and went to get my sleeping clothes.

"Kendra is wearing red," he said simply and a sudden burst of jealousy startled me. Dang it! Why did I care? And why did he have to tell me what she was wearing? Kendra was the last person on earth I wanted to hear about. He could hear or feel my thoughts. Getting a handle on my emotions would be really good about now.

"That's great. I'm sure she'll be stunning." I managed to say with only a very small amount of venom dripping from my words.

"I hate the color red almost as much as I hate blond hair," he said with an amused tone. I started to respond but stopped myself. I didn't believe him but what was the point in calling him on it? It wasn't as if I couldn't see him and Kendra together all day long every day. It was as if he constantly jabbed a fist through my stomach every time he touched her or whispered in her ear. I turned my back on him and walked over to my jewelry box to find jewelry to match. It was better than thinking about Kendra in a red dress with Dank's hands all over her.

Warmth pressed against my back causing a shiver to run through my body. I reached for the edge of the dresser to keep from losing my balance and crumpling to the floor. I knew Dank was behind me. Even though I didn't understand it, I knew only his touch would cause this strong reaction. I let my head fall back onto the solid warmth of his chest.

"She means nothing to me." Dank's voice sent tingles down my neck and across my chest. "I would never lie to you, Pagan," he said urgently against my ear. I opened my eyes to gaze up at him, wanting to see the blue of his eyes. His lips touched the tip of my ear and made a trail up my face. Both his hands gripped my waist pulling me hard up against his body. "You tempt me. I can't be tempted. I'm not made to be tempted but you, Pagan Moore, you tempt me. From the moment I came for you I was drawn in. Everything about you..." One of his hands left my waist and moved up to gently caress my arm. "You make me crazy with need. With want. I didn't understand it at first. But now I know. It's your soul calling to me. Souls mean nothing to me. They aren't supposed to. But yours has become my obsession." He lowered his head to my shoulder and kissed the curve of my neck. His hand moved over to slip beneath my shirt and the heat from his palm rested on my bare stomach. A pulse of warmth surged through me and he pressed me tightly against him to keep me from falling. "I want to kill that boy every time I see his hands on you." He kissed a path up my neck and I arched my neck in response to give him better access. Nothing had ever felt like this. His touch was like a drug. "I want to rip his arms from his body so he can't touch you again." A low, familiar growl vibrated against my back. "But I can't have you, Pagan. You're not meant for me." His voice sounded tortured. I wanted to comfort him. He'd claimed me too. Somehow, he'd walked into my world and become the center of it. He was all I wanted. I started to tell him just how much he meant to me when he picked me up and laid me carefully on the bed, hovering over me. I reached up to him wanting to feel his body against mine again but he pulled away.

"Please," I whispered.

Dank closed his eyes tightly as if he were in pain. "I can't, Pagan. It would destroy us both." And then he was gone.

# Chapter Eight

Leif kissed my cheek before leaving me at the door of my English Literature class. I'd started riding to school with him every morning. Each morning it had been increasingly more difficult to leave the presence of Dank and walk into the realness of Leif. After sleeping with Dank's voice singing in my ear all night, I seemed to crave his presence even more. An intimacy now existed between us. After having his hands on my body and his lips against my skin, nothing had been the same. He'd lain down beside me last night and held me against him as I fell asleep. I needed Dank. The words he whispered in my ear at night assured me he wanted me too. He needed me but he was letting some unseen barrier stand between us.

I started over to my desk when I noticed the one behind it remained empty. It was Dank's usual spot. He would be here soon. I settled into my desk and went ahead and found where we had left off on Friday. Every time I saw someone step in the door from my peripheral vision I glanced up to see if it was Dank. Kendra's bubbly voice and bouncing blond head came through the door, and he followed her, carrying her books. My gut twisted into a painful knot. I forced myself to look away. He'd said he didn't like blonds yesterday but the way he gazed down at her affectionately said something else entirely. I stared down at the open book in front of me, not taking in any of the words. I was waiting for Dank to sit down behind me. He never did. Mr. Brown walked into the room whistling and smiled at the class.

"Ah, good to see such excited faces this morning. Isn't English Literature a joy? What better way to wake up?" he asked in a jovial tone. He turned and wrote this week's assignment on the board. I wanted to glance back and see where Dank sat today but I refused to let myself. I could feel him staring at me, no doubt waiting to see if I would search for him. Well, I wouldn't give him the satisfaction. Besides, he was probably playing with those long blond locks of hair he claimed to hate. He'd whispered that he wanted me. That I was the only one he'd ever needed.

"Can anyone tell me one of the major themes we learned while studying *The Eumeides*?" Wanting desperately to get my mind off of Dank, I held my hand in the air. Mr. Brown smiled and nodded, "Alright then, Miss Moore."

71

"Conflict between the old and the new, between savagery and civilization, between the primal and the rational," I replied and Mr. Brown clapped his hands.

"Very good. Now, an example of this theme?" He glanced around the room and I raised my hand again. Mr. Brown raised his eyebrows, no doubt in surprise at my sudden desire to join in on class participation. "Pagan?"

"The progression of old to new gods. Zeus overthrew the older generations of gods, and among those ancient deities were the Furies. The Furies became outcasts." I stopped, not wanting to go any further.

"Good, good, very good. Now, can someone other than Pagan please explain where Apollo fell into this?"

The room went quiet and someone giggled. "Kendra maybe you could help us out with an answer," Mr. Brown aimed his frown back toward the apparent source of the giggle.

"No sir, I have a life outside school work. Not all of us spend all of our extra time studying and tutoring in order to snag a boyfriend."

Another burst of giggles erupted and Mr. Brown tilted his head to one side. "I don't believe that's the proper answer, Kendra, you'll receive a low mark for today's participation. Now, can anyone else tell me or shall I ask Miss. Moore again to help us out?"

"Apollo is a symbol for the male, the rational, the young, and the civilized. The Furies represent the female, the violent, the old, and the primal. *Aeschylus* captures a mythical moment in history, one in which the world was torn between a savage and archaic past and the bold new order of Greek civilization, the young Olympian gods, and rationality. The difficulty of the struggle between these two worlds is dramatized by the cycle of violence in the House of Atreus and the clash between Apollo and the Furies."

No one giggled after Dank finished. There was no question in my mind, he'd done that for me. I turned this time to find him exactly where I'd expected. He was seated behind Kendra whose expression was so pinched you would have thought someone just slapped her. He gave me a wink and flashed that one perfect dimple. I couldn't wipe the grin off my face.

"Very well done, Mr. Walker. Now, let us hope the rest of you grasp this piece of literature as well as Pagan and Dank because today we embark upon a journey even further into this world created by Aeschylus."

Having Dank answer more elaborately than I to show there was nothing wrong with knowing the answers helped me stay focused on Mr. Brown's discussion. Still, Dank remained at the forefront of my mind.

At the end of the day I reached into my locker and pulled out the books I needed for homework. Two warm hands slid around my waist.

"I missed you," Leif whispered in my ear and I turned my head back to him and smiled.

"I've missed you, too, but aren't you supposed to be at practice?"

He shrugged. "I was on my way when I thought about you standing at your locker and how easy it would be to take a detour to come see you."

"I'm glad you did. Now get to the field house before the coach makes you run suicides for being late."

He bent down and kissed me gently on the lips. "I'll see you tonight," he said, stepping back and turning to jog toward the front doors. I stood watching him until he was out of sight, and then I sighed and turned back to close my locker. Today had been trying and I just wanted to go home.

A shiver ran down my spine and I froze. It wasn't a good shiver like the ones Dank caused. It was another kind of shiver. The kind I remembered from once before. Fear caused my heart to pound wildly inside my chest. I took two deep breaths before turning around slowly. The blond soul stood watching me from across the hallway. She was studying me as she had done the last time I'd seen her. I swallowed against the nausea of overwhelming fear rising in my throat, almost suffocating me. I was alone in an empty hallway. Why had I not left with Leif? I backed up toward the front doors but they were too far away to make me feel safe. She laughed, that tinkling sound sending chills down my arms. Every step I took back she took forward.

"Leave me alone." I grimaced at the weakness of my demand. It was obvious I was terrified.

She raised her eyebrows in surprise. "I can't," she said as she approached. I thought of turning and running but I knew she would catch me easily enough.

"Go away or I'll tell Dank," I said with very little conviction as my voice wavered. Her tinkling laughter rang out again.

"He is currently busy with the blond one. I don't know why he is putting this off," she said when she was only a few steps away from me. I pulled my book bag closer to my chest and fought the urge to scream.

"Dank," I whispered past the terror squeezing my throat, hoping somehow he would hear me. The blond glanced around as if panicked, but only for a moment. Then her angelic smile returned. "Like I said, he is busy." She reached out a hand to touch me and I cringed, expecting the cold feel of her hands.

"I wouldn't do that if I were you." Dank's voice made me go weak with relief. His protective arms wrapped around me and I sank against him.

"Leave this alone. It is for no one else to decide." Her hauntingly-beautiful eyes glared up at him with a fierceness that chilled me. "It was never your decision to make. The rules are as they have always been. It will have to be."

His arms tightened around me. "You're going to leave and stay away from her. If you come near her again I won't forgive easily." A flash of fear crossed her eyes and she stepped back farther from us and then she was gone.

My legs went limp with relief. Dank pulled me up closer against him to keep me from sinking to the floor. "Did she touch you?" he asked in a cold voice I hadn't been expecting. I shook my head, not sure my voice was ready to work. I turned my head to look back at him. He was staring down the hall. I could hear a low sound in his chest as he snarled at the now empty hallway.

"Come on, I'm taking you home."

I let him keep his arm wrapped around my waist to steady me as he led me out into the parking lot. He stopped in front of topless black jeep and opened the passenger side door. I had no idea he even had a vehicle but then again nothing should surprise me at this point. He lifted me into the seat like I was a child and walked around to climb into the driver's seat.

"How did you know?" I asked once we were out of the school parking lot. He glanced over at me.

"I heard your fear...and then I heard my name and the desperation in it was..." he stopped and glared back at the road. I waited in silence for him to finish but he remained silent.

"It was what?" I asked in a whisper.

He let out a frustrated sigh. "Terrifying. Knowing you were that scared...hearing the fear was unlike anything I've ever felt. I was ready to cease the existence of whatever was hurting you. Then I saw her and knew it was something I couldn't control without, without...doing something that would be close to unbearable to me, but more bearable than the alternative."

I heard his words but none of them made sense. I frowned and shook my head, wanting to understand and he reached over and took my hand in his. "Pagan, please don't ask for what I can't give you. I can give you anything but the answers to those questions."

I closed my eyes and turned my face away from him. I wanted to hate him for not telling me who he was or what he was. I wanted to understand him, to understand this, but he wouldn't or couldn't tell me anything.

The moment the jeep stopped outside my house, I grabbed my bag and hopped out. I needed distance. Nothing about this made any sense and I wanted to understand. I turned to slam the door and saw Dank standing at his jeep with a defeated expression. I paused. The urge to call out to him was so strong, but I resisted and closed the door softly. I could not understand why he refused to explain what was happening to me. I wanted to hate him but he'd claimed a part of my soul and there was nothing I could do to stop my feelings for him. His appearance in my life had started all of this craziness. He offered to give me anything in the world other than the answers I wanted and needed. I threw my book bag down on the kitchen counter and plopped onto a bar stool. Tonight Leif would come over and we would work on his speech for this week. It would all be very normal teenage stuff. I would pretend I didn't live in a world of haunting paranormal activity. Maybe I would even cook him dinner. All very normal, all very real.

I finished cutting up the quesadillas as the doorbell rang. I grabbed the plate and sat it down on the kitchen table on my way to the door.

Leif grinned and stepped inside. "Whatever I smell is heavenly. Please tell me it's for me, because I'm starving." I stood on my tippy toes and kissed him chastely on the lips before heading back to the kitchen to get drinks from the fridge.

"I made quesadillas tonight. Do you want sour cream or guacamole?" I asked, turning back to look at him.

"Sour cream," he replied. All very normal. No crazy blond souls trying to scare the bejesus out of me. Just me and my boyfriend, working on our homework.

"Okay, we eat first and then work on your speech about—what is it this week?" I asked as I sat the drinks, sour cream, and guacamole down on the table.

"The importance of a college degree," he answered, smiling with a quesadilla already half way to his mouth.

I sat down across from him. "That should be easy enough."

Leif nodded and took another bite of a sour cream-smothered quesadilla. Movement from across the room caught my attention. Startled, I started to stand up, ready to bolt when Dank sauntered into the room. He saluted me and walked up the stairs to my room. I watched him go, feeling sadness overwhelm me. I'd been rude this evening and he'd come to me anyway. Secretly I'd been worrying he wouldn't show tonight after the way I walked away from him. I glanced over at Leif who was taking a swig of his drink.

"Um, I need to run upstairs and get something, I mean do something. I'll be right back, uh, go on ahead and eat until you're full." He smiled and took another bite. I headed back up the stairs and walked into my room, immediately glancing toward the bed to find it empty. Instead of lounging on my bed I found him in my chair with the guitar in his hands.

"Hey," I said, not sure what I'd come up here to say. His grin showcasing his dimple made me shiver.

"Hey," he replied as he strummed at the guitar. I stood for a moment and listened to him play the tune I'd heard him sing at night when he thought I was asleep. I sat down on my bed and watched him play. He was a contradiction. A soul who wasn't a soul but could do things a soul could do. A rock star that was supposed to be in a band that he was never with. I hadn't thought of any of this before now.

"Dank, why're you here? If you sing in a band, I mean, what brought you here?" He smiled sadly and stared back down at the guitar in his hands.

"I do sing with the band when they have gigs. Cold Soul isn't a headliner yet. I can come and go easily, Pagan, you know that. Keeping up with my other life is easy enough." Of course he had it all under control. He was a jack of all trades: High school heart throb, singer in a band, the ability to become like a ghost and my bodyguard. His dark blue eyes glanced back up at me. "Why are you up here when Mr. Wonderful is downstairs?" he asked and the strumming ceased.

I shrugged. "I don't know, you just looked like you might need me," I said, hating the way the words sounded. He sat his guitar down and stood up. I watched as he knelt down right in front of me. I sat hypnotized as he traced my jaw line with his finger and then gently touched my lips. Desire surged through my body so strongly I grabbed a handful of the quilt I was sitting on.

"I need you. Never doubt my need for you. But right now is not the time to explore my need. You have a love-struck boy downstairs needing your assistance with his homework," he said gently as he stood up and stepped back away from me before turning his back on me and vanishing. I stood in my empty bedroom and took several deep breaths to steady my racing heart before heading back downstairs to help Leif write his essay. I realized my hands were trembling when I closed my bedroom door behind me. If just his touch made me react so strongly, how much more would his actual lips on mine affect me? I closed my eyes against the need coursing through me and mentally shook myself.

Later that night, after my shower, I walked into my room and found Dank already sitting in the corner chair, strumming on his guitar. He didn't glance up at me. Disappointed that he didn't seem to want to finish what we'd started earlier, I pulled the covers back on my bed and slipped inside. I wanted to ask him why he'd left but he didn't appear to want to talk to me. Had he seen Leif kiss me goodnight downstairs? Was he upset? I hadn't heard the familiar growl that normally meant Dank was witnessing Leif kiss me. It no longer made me smile. It chipped away at my heart a little. I didn't like the thought of hurting him.

"Dank," I whispered in the darkness but he didn't look up at me. His voice joined the music and I fought the urge to close my eyes and drift off into the sleep the comfort of his voice seemed to induce. I watched him, silently pleading with him to look at me. Had I hurt him?

"Close your eyes, Pagan, and stop worrying about me. The life I've placed myself into is mine to endure. You have no reason to worry that you cause me pain. You do the exact opposite to me than what you fear."

I watched him, not sure what he meant by my doing the opposite.

"As for the kissing, you're right, I don't like to see it. If I choose to watch it, it's my fault. I'll deal with it." He lifted his head from the guitar in his hands this time and stared straight at me. "The emotion he evokes in you is not strong. There is only comfort, not passion, running through your thoughts when he holds you." His attention turned back to the guitar in his hands.

"Will you hold me tonight?" I asked. His beautiful eyes lifted and gazed at me with so much emotion it took my breath away.

"There is nothing I'd rather do, but tonight my strength is weak. I can't hold you right now. I want too much. Please, Pagan, tonight just sleep." I watched him strum the chords on his guitar until my eyes grew heavy. Dank was right. Leif was my safe haven. My touch-stone for normalcy. He was a friend. It was Dank who consumed me.

# Chapter Nine

"It doesn't look a thing like our gym! GAH! How fantabulous does this place look?" Miranda swirled around to smile at us, extremely pleased with the decorations in the gym. She was right. They had done an excellent job making the gym into an oceanic starry night.

"It is impressive," I agreed as Leif's arm pulled me closer to his side.

"Do you feel like dancing?" he asked as the music changed from a slow song to Lady Gaga's *Just Dance.*

I shook my head and glanced over toward the tables. "Can we sit this one out? I'm not sure my rib is up for that kind of movement." He steered me toward the tables as Miranda grabbed Wyatt and pulled him onto the dance floor. I laughed at Wyatt's pained expression and turned to say something to Leif when I realized his attention was focused on the entrance. There was a scowl on his face. Dank had just walked in, looking breathtaking in a pair of jeans, a black t-shirt, and army boots. It took me a moment to take my eyes off of him to notice Kendra was plastered to his side. She had been melted and poured into the red dress she had on. Either that or it wasn't really a dress at all but something she had painted on her body. Jealousy flared up in my chest at the sight of Dank's arm around her waist. I glanced back up at Leif who was still staring at the couple with dislike.

"Are you okay?" I asked, and he jerked his gaze away from Kendra and Dank.

He nodded, stopped, and studied me a moment. "You have some classes with Dank, and you've spoken to him a few times, haven't you?" I nodded, not sure where this was going so I waited for more. "Something about him concerns me. Kendra has some issues that make her unstable and I'm beginning to worry that Dank isn't the kind of guy she needs. He seems dark and sinister."

My jealousy was forgotten and quickly replaced by anger. Leif thought Dank wasn't good enough for Kendra, the town slut? I managed to hold an angry burst of laughter in and I glared out at the dance floor wishing I could somehow get away. I needed to calm down.

"What? You look mad. Don't get me wrong I don't like Kendra,

Pagan. That isn't what this is about." He reached for my other arm and pulled me around to face him. His earlier hostile expression toward Dank had vanished. Now he was worried and for the first time I didn't care about easing his concern. "Look at me. I don't want her. You're all I want. I love you Pagan. It isn't like that with Kendra. I just don't want her hurt. She has—"

"Issues, yeah, I heard you," I said, cutting him off before I forgot myself and made a scene. I took a deep breath reminding myself I was taking this personally because of my feelings for Dank. "Look, if Dank Walker has any interest in Kendra then she should count herself lucky. From what I know of him he is intelligent, honest, talented, and compassionate."

I glared back at Leif who seemed to be taking in my words. I wanted to say more and continue defending Dank but I knew I'd said enough. "I need something to drink. I'll be right back," I said before turning and walking away. It was abrupt but I needed to put some space between my anger and Leif.

Miranda waved at me as I passed by where she and Wyatt were dancing. I forced a smile but kept walking. Kendra's skin-tight red dress caught my eye and I turned to see her wrapped around Dank, laughing and dancing in such a way that would have the chaperones on her within seconds. Jealousy knotted in my stomach at the way Dank held and touched her in ways he'd never touched me. I didn't head toward the refreshment table. Instead, I headed for the back doors. I needed to get away from Leif and Dank. I paused at the door. Being alone in the dark might not be such a good idea. Kendra's laughter rang in my ears and I decided right now, I would rather face the touchy creepy blond soul than watch Dank holding Kendra.

The night breeze had cooled down in the last couple of weeks. I wrapped my arms around my waist and walked toward the deserted football field. The emotions churning inside me gave me a sense of bravado. I walked on, away from the music and laughter. I thought back to last summer at my aunt's ranch and how easy things had been. I'd spent my time riding horses and helping my aunt deal with the death of my uncle. Mom had suggested I go visit her so she wouldn't be alone. I'd agreed to go, thinking that being away from this town and my memories of Jay would help. It had, in a sense. After a few weeks, I'd come to realize Jay and I were never meant to be. Another pro about being on the ranch had been the wandering souls had seemed to be sparse. It had been a brief reprieve from my life. However, the last few weeks of the summer, I'd looked forward to coming home. I glanced back at the gym and thought of how crazy things had gotten since my return.

"Why aren't you inside dancing with your date?" Dank's voice broke the silence and I turned to see him leaning up against the cement wall of the stadium. I shrugged and ducked my head as if studying my feet. I didn't want him to see the hurt or jealousy in my eyes. It was bad enough he probably already knew. "He's looking rather forlorn sitting at a table all alone," Dank said quietly into the night. A flicker of guilt deep in my stomach wasn't enough to send me back inside. I shrugged again and didn't meet his probing gaze. He chuckled and the low, sexy sound sent a shiver through me. "So, have you decided to try the ignoring me thing again, to see if I go away?" he asked with a touch of humor in his voice.

I bit my lip to keep from smiling and shook my head no. "I know that doesn't work with you."

"Why are you out here, Pagan? What's wrong?" he asked quietly. I reluctantly glanced up at him. He was so incredibly beautiful standing with his arms crossed in front of his chest. The dark hair that curled at the ends seemed to dance in the breeze.

"Nothing that concerns you," I lied. He tilted his head to one side and flashed me a wicked grin.

"Really?"

I nodded. "Really."

His hands fell to his sides as he stepped away from the wall and took a step toward me. "Seeing me dance with Kendra doesn't bother you?" he asked in a husky whisper. I shook my head and looked away from him, refusing to step back from his nearness. His eyes bore down on me so intensely it was as if he were actually touching me. My heart started beating hard against my ribs and I looked at him. His eyes flickered from my dress back to my face. "I knew pale pink would suit you. Most girls can't pull it off but on you it's perfect."

I swallowed, afraid my heart was about to pound right out of my chest. I didn't want to think about the way his gaze made every cell in my body come alive.

"You think I don't want to touch you the way I touch Kendra. You're right." His words washed over me like ice water and I stepped back away from him as if he'd just slapped me. My pounding heart constricted and I took a quick intake of air, afraid, for a moment, that I wouldn't be able to breathe. His hand reached out, grabbed mine, and pulled me up against him. "When I touch Kendra I mentally cringe at having to continue to pull off the farce of being interested in her."

I stopped trying to pull my hand out of his and stared up at him. This sounded like something I wanted to hear.

"When I can't control my need for you and allow myself to touch you it ignites a monster inside of me that I'm afraid I'll lose control over. You make me feel things I've never felt before. Something happens," he paused and lowered his gaze from my eyes to my lips, "when I'm near you like this." He touched my lips with his fingertip and I trembled. He closed his eyes as if in pain. "And when you react the way you do, I feel the clawing inside me to take what I want."

He opened his eyes and stared at me with an intensity that would have frightened me had I not trusted him so completely. "You're the one thing I want the most in the world yet the one thing I cannot have. Because to have you completely would be impossible. You can't go where I walk." He stopped and cradled my face in his hands. "The purpose of my existence is not to have a mate. It is lonely and cold. Until now it has been all I've known. Then you became the appointed and everything changed." He dropped his hands from me and backed away as a pained desperation clouded his eyes. "Go, Pagan. Run, please, run. I am not what you think I am. I am not 'intelligent, honest, talented, and compassionate' although hearing you say those words in my defense felt like warm liquid pouring through my cold veins. You want to know what I am and I can't tell you. If you knew, I wouldn't have to beg you to run."

He snarled and turned away from me, stalking off toward the darkness. I couldn't let him go. I ran after him and he turned abruptly. His angry glare stunned me and I froze. The anger seemed to leave him immediately and a tortured expression came over his perfectly-chiseled features. I gasped at the transformation.

"I don't care what you are," I said, taking a step toward him. "You can't scare me off and I'm not running away. What is it the song you sing to me says? *Yet you stay. Holding on to me, yet you stay, reaching out a hand that I push away. The cold is not meant for you yet you stay, you stay, you stay. When I know it's not right for you'.*" I repeated his words to him in the darkness. His face contorted in pain.

"Go, Pagan. Now. I can't control myself much longer," he whispered into the darkness.

I took another step toward him. A low growl erupted from his chest and he seized me in one swift movement. His mouth found mine instantly. His teeth nipped my bottom lip and then he gently swiped his tongue over the bite. My first taste of him sent my world spinning. Somehow I'd known it would be like this.    I grabbed handfuls of Dank's shirt. I needed to keep him here against me, finally allowing me to have what I'd been craving. His arms tightened around me and I heard a moan in the darkness but I wasn't sure if it was his or mine. My purpose in life was complete. There was nothing else I wanted or desired more than this. There was a darkness pulling at us, I couldn't grasp what it was exactly but even through the haze of pleasure I knew it was there. Dank trailed kisses down my neck and murmured words I didn't understand. I released his shirt to grab his face, hungrily bringing his mouth back to mine. His hands slowly ran up my back and slipped over my ribs. My breath hitched as his thumbs grazed the bottom of my bra. Dank tore his mouth from mine, panting loudly. It thrilled me to see him as needy as I was for this.

"I can't, Pagan. I want this so damn bad. But I can't."

In the blink of an eye I was alone, sitting on the cold grass in the middle of the football field. My breathing was ragged and my head was spinning. Where was Dank? My eyes searched frantically through the darkness for him. Why had he left me? The feeling of euphoria had disappeared with him and my body ached from its loss.

"Pagan?" a worried voice called from behind me. I didn't turn because I recognized Leif's voice. He had come to find me and here I sat in my pale pink dress, bought for another guy, in the middle of a deserted football field. Maybe I was going crazy. He knelt down in front of me with fear and worry etched on his handsome face.

"God, you scared me. I came outside looking for you and I saw you faint or fall...are you okay? I'm sorry, Pagan, I didn't mean to upset you. Please, please forgive me." He was holding my hands in his, yet the warmth from his body couldn't penetrate the cold that was seeping through me. I stared up at him, knowing I had to say something. But what could I say?

"It's fine. I just don't feel well. My head." I touched my head for effect. "I'm sorry, but I just want to go home." He stood and helped me up, wrapping his arm around my waist as a means of support. We walked in silence across the field and into the dark parking lot. I wasn't sure if he was angry or hurt but right now I just needed to be alone. My mind couldn't seem to wrap itself around what had just happened and I knew deep down I was hoping Dank would be in my room waiting for me.

We didn't speak the entire trip home. I hated the silence but there was no way to explain what had happened. When he pulled into my driveway he turned the car off and then glanced over at me.

"I hope you can forgive me for upsetting you." He let out a sigh of disgust. "Here I am all worried about Kendra's personal life and I end up hurting the only girl I've ever loved with my stupidity." He stopped and shook his head. "You're still healing from something I caused. You never complain about it but I know you're still dealing with after effects from your wreck. I don't know if I'm going to be able to forgive myself for letting my stupid mouth upset you so much that you..." he motioned with his hand as if toward the football field miles away, "...go off alone and faint from the stress I inflicted."

I couldn't take him blaming himself for what happened anymore. I forced myself to snap out of my haze and take his hand. "Leif, listen to me. What happened tonight is not your fault. I'm not entirely sure what happened myself, but no one is to blame, except maybe me. You had nothing, and I mean nothing, to do with it."

The small flicker of relief in his eyes wasn't strong enough to compensate for his tortured expression. He pulled my hand up to his mouth and kissed it. "I love you, Pagan Moore." He had been saying those three words a lot tonight. I knew I couldn't say the words he wanted to hear. Leif was special to me but I didn't love him, at least not the way he wanted me to. I did the only thing I could think of. I leaned over and kissed him softly on the lips, and then turned, and got out of the car. I headed for the door without a backwards glance.

My bedroom was empty but somehow I'd known it would be. Something had happened tonight. I didn't know what it was but I knew it was important. I walked over to the chair where Dank spent his nights and I curled up on it. He wouldn't come tonight. I needed to be close to him and this seemed like the only way. The silence seemed to cut through me like a knife and warm tears trickled down my face. I missed his voice filling my room with warmth. I didn't want him to leave me. The fear that he was gone hurt so much it constricted my airways. The blond soul that had frightened me no longer seemed important. The absence of Dank made my chest ache. I couldn't take the silence anymore so I began to sing softly in the darkness.

"*Yet you stay. Holding on to me, yet you stay, reaching out a hand that I push away. The cold is not meant for you yet you stay, you stay, you stay. When I know it's not right for you.*"

# Chapter Ten

He didn't come back. I spent the entire weekend closed up in my bedroom waiting for him but he never came. I'd gotten up Monday morning and dressed with such desperation I almost ran out to my car to rush off to school. When my mother asked, "Is Leif not picking you up today?" I stopped with my hand on the doorknob, unsure how to answer. I'd let his calls go to voicemail most of the weekend. After listening to his pleading messages I'd finally called him and reassured him I was just in bed, sick. He would be expecting to take me to school this morning. I forced myself to sit down and eat my breakfast while I waited ten more minutes for Leif to arrive. Somehow, I managed to maintain the appearance of patience until I walked in the front doors of the school. I couldn't feel him. He wasn't here. Kendra's pouty, red lips reassured me that he wasn't hiding from me. He just wasn't here. Each class that went by without him felt like an ever-expanding black hole in my world. Leif watched me with a mix of concern and frustration I knew he was trying to conceal. Once the last bell rang I walked out of the library and headed for home. I needed him to be there.

But he wasn't. He stayed away for two more days.

The moment I walked into English Literature on Thursday, I felt him. The tingling warmth I'd grown accustomed to was strong due to its four day absence. I looked to the back of the room and there he sat, giving Kendra his crooked grin while tracing her jaw line with his fingertip. She giggled and he leaned closer and whispered something in her ear that caused her to throw her head back and laugh. She glanced my way and smirked triumphantly. I glanced from her to Dank who seemed to not see me at all. He was watching her, smiling seductively. He had kissed me and left me alone, confused, and then vanished for four days. Now, it was as if nothing had ever happened.

I stared at him, willing him to look at me, to acknowledge my presence. He didn't. Unable to watch anymore, I turned around and left the room. Leif was still standing outside the door, where I'd left him. He was talking to Justin and glanced back at me with a surprised smile.

"Hey, did you forget something?" he asked, reaching for my hand. I shook my head, afraid the huge gaping hole Dank had just torn in my heart was visible to the world. I walked up to Leif and wrapped my arms around his waist. His arms encircled me instantly.

"I'll talk to you later, man," I heard him say to Justin over my head.

"What's wrong?" he whispered in my ear as he continued to hold me. I wanted to weep because I didn't love him. Leif loved me and he would be easy to love. He would never hurt me the way Dank just did. He was so good and honest. Why couldn't I love him instead? I held on tighter to him, afraid he could hear my thoughts and would back away from me any moment. However, Leif couldn't hear my fears.

He pulled me closer and began rubbing small circles on my back with his hand. Tears sprang into my eyes and I hated to cry in his arms over another guy. Leif deserved someone who could love him. I'd once hated him because I thought he believed he was too good for me. Now, I hated myself because I knew he was too good for me. I didn't deserve him, yet I held onto him anyway. I may not love him, but I needed him. He had no idea my insides felt as if they were being ripped from my body because of the way someone or something else rejected me.

"Mr. Brown, Pagan doesn't feel well. She needs to go to the nurse's office. If she goes home, I'll make sure to bring her excuse back to you myself." Leif explained to my teacher as he held me.

"Very well, you're taking her then?" Mr. Brown's voice sounded concerned.

"Yes, sir." The door closed and the hallway became quiet. I didn't want to see a nurse but I knew I couldn't stand in the hallway all day letting Leif hold me. Though I was pretty positive if I wanted him to do so, he would. I stepped back just enough to gaze up at his face. His face was a mask of concern as he wiped a tear from my cheek.

"What's wrong, Pagan?" he asked quietly.

I managed a weak smile. "I think my feeling bad just got to me. I want to feel good again. This weekend was miserable," I admitted, needing to add some truth to what I was saying.

He nodded and pulled me back into his arms. "I'm sorry for my part in this. I can't stand seeing you cry. It kills me," he said softly and squeezed me. Leif was my link to the real world and my source of comfort, especially now my heart felt broken beyond repair. What scared me the most was the fact that my heart had been shattered by someone I didn't even know.

I went to the nurse but only remained in there long enough for English Literature to end. Once I knew it would be safe to head to Algebra II, I assured Nurse Tavers I felt much better and wanted to go to class. Algebra II happened to be the only class I didn't share with Dank or Kendra. I could make it through this one. Leif would be with me in World History so Dank's presence would be easier to ignore.

I stepped into the hall and the eerie warning in my head that someone was watching me made the hairs on my arms stand up. I glanced both ways down the empty hallway but no one was there. Fear seemed to clog my throat and I forced myself to take a calming breath before heading toward Algebra II with my pass from Nurse Tavers. I walked faster than normal, wanting to be around other people. Being alone in the hallway brought back frightening memories. Especially now, I wasn't sure Dank would come to my rescue. He wouldn't even look at me, so why would he come to me if a soul haunted me? The sensation that someone was there watching me intensified the farther down the hall I walked. Why did Algebra II have to be at the very end of the hall? I peeked back over my shoulder and still the hallway remained empty. A chill ran up my spine and I broke into a run. I couldn't see her but I knew she was there. My heart pounded in my chest. I kept my eyes on the door to my Algebra II class. It still seemed so far away, yet I knew if I screamed someone would hear me. The coldness grew stronger and the air had grown thick, making it harder to breathe. I needed to stop running so I could force oxygen into my lungs but then she would have me alone that much longer.

A door opened just as my vision started becoming hazy from lack of oxygen and air immediately filled my burning lungs. The chill disappeared. I dropped my books and put my hands on my knees, gasping for more air, drawing it in and trying to steady my racing heart. Footsteps startled me and I jerked up ready to run again when I saw Dank walking away. Whatever had been after me fled because of him. Lucky for me she didn't realize Dank didn't care about keeping me safe anymore. My heart no longer raced from fear but ached from the pain of rejection. I picked my books up off the ground and watched Dank's retreating form one more time before heading into my classroom.


"If you aren't ready to start on my speech, I'm not in a hurry," Leif leaned down and whispered in my ear. We ordered pizza and cuddled on the couch to watch television.

The truth of the matter was, I wasn't in the mood to work on his speech. All I really wanted to do was enjoy the small measure of warmth from being in his arms. Sitting on the couch cuddling with my boyfriend helped me keep my fear at bay. When Leif left, I would have to go to my room alone. The thought of facing my room after my experience in the hall today terrified me. Seeing Dank saunter away from me as if he were just another guy without a care in the world, while I stood bent over gasping for air had left me with a feeling of despair. I reached down and took Leif's hand in mine. He was here. Granted he was no protection against psycho souls. Only Dank could stop that... that... whatever she was. But Dank wasn't here. Leif was all I had and I wanted to bask in his presence a while longer. Leif held my hand in his and we sat in silence. I wasn't even sure what we were watching. He would laugh out loud at times and the sound of it made me smile. I enjoyed seeing him happy. Sometimes I forgot what happy felt like. The ringing of his phone broke into my thoughts and I jumped. I was on edge tonight.

He grinned. "It's my phone, not the fire alarm. Jeesh, you're jumpy tonight." He reached into his pocket and slid it out.

"Hello?" he paused, "I'm at Pagan's right now....I realize that, but I'm busy....We haven't finished it yet." Leif glanced down at me apologetically. "Okay, I'm on my way," he said, frowning as he closed his phone. "That was my dad. He needs me to ride with him to drop mom's car off at the mechanic's. They're going to work on it first thing in the morning. He can't go to bed until he has dropped it off and he's beat after working a double shift at the station."

I sat up and forced a smile. My mother wasn't home yet and the thought of being alone made me want to curl up in a ball and cry. "Oh, yeah, um, go on. We can work on the speech tomorrow."

He frowned and slipped a hand into my hair, brushing his thumb against my ear. "You look uptight. I hate to leave you all wound up."

I smiled and shrugged. "I probably just need some sleep," I lied, hoping he bought it. He bent down and kissed me softly. I slid my hands behind his neck and deepened the kiss. Leif took my face in his hands and tilted it to fit his perfectly. I soaked in the comfort of his closeness and his warmth. I knew I needed to let him go so he could go help his dad but I held on tighter. Letting him go meant he would leave and I would be alone. I pressed up against him without thinking about how my need for comfort would be misinterpreted for passion. A moan came from Leif's chest and he gently pushed me back on the couch and covered me with his body.

We'd never let things go this far before. Dank always stood there, somewhere in the middle: an unseen force that had me holding Leif back at a distance. It would be wrong now to allow things to go any further. Leading Leif to believe we could go further in our relationship wasn't fair to either of us. Dank would always be there in my mind. Leif deserved more than being second best. Even now as he pressed against me and his breathing sounded ragged, I felt nothing but security. His hand slid beneath my shirt and I knew it was time to stop. Just as he brushed the underside of my bra I broke away from the kiss.

"No," I whispered and his hand slowly retreated. His breathing sounded labored and I could feel his heart thumping against mine. Slowly he sat up and reached for my hand to pull me up too. He ran a hand through his tousled blond hair and laughed shakily.

"Wow," he said, smiling. I wasn't sure what to say because "wow" wasn't what I felt. "I'm sorry, I got carried away," he apologized staring down at my shirt that was still hitched up just above my belly button. I tugged it down and smiled reassuringly at him. It wasn't as if he'd just attempted to rape me.

"Don't apologize. We just needed to stop. Your dad is waiting."

Leif nodded, his expression still a little glazed over, and stood up. He slipped his jacket on and grabbed his books and keys.

"Are you going to be okay until your mom gets home?" he asked.

I wanted to laugh at the answer to that question. Instead, I nodded and smiled. It wasn't like I could tell him a deranged soul wanted to kill me for reasons I didn't understand.

The door closing behind Leif made the lead weight on my chest vibrate. I thought of going outside and standing in my yard so I could see other houses lit up and people inside them. Somehow, knowing other people where inside them sounded safe. I glanced back at the stairs and the thought of going up to my room made me tremble. I walked over and stood at the front door. I could stand here until my mom got home. If anything showed up I could take off running down the street and screaming. Granted, everyone would think I was mental, but still it would draw some attention.

"I don't think such drastic measures will be necessary. Go on up to bed Pagan, I'll be here." I turned at the sound of Dank's voice. Relief and anger washed over me simultaneously. I wanted to throw my arms around him but then I also wanted to punch him in his perfect nose.

"I'd prefer you do neither. Just go to bed." His cold tone hurt worse than the fear. He wasn't looking at me, but instead at a sports magazine Leif had left behind. His boots were propped up on the table as he reclined in a chair. Tears burned my eyes, but I would not cry in front of him. That was one humiliation I refused to give him. Instead I ran up the stairs.

The hot water washed away my tears as I stood in the shower much longer than necessary. In here my sobs were camouflaged. Once the tears stopped falling and all that was left was a hollow ache, I turned off the water, stepped out onto the white fluffy rug and wrapped a towel around me. I studied the girl in the mirror. Her eyes were red and puffy. No amount of hot water could wash away the sadness they reflected. He was here and I was safe. I had something to be thankful for. Why he was here I didn't have the courage to ask him. I did not want him to see me cry. I didn't want him to know I'd just spent thirty minutes in the shower crying over him. He may have stolen my heart or had he taken my soul? I couldn't be sure but I refused to let him have my pride too.

I wrapped the towel tighter around me and headed for my bedroom. I stepped inside knowing it would be empty. Dank didn't want to be anywhere near me. A small part of me had hoped to find him sitting in the corner chair with his guitar in his hands. Fresh tears sprang to my eyes. I needed to get control over this agony or whatever it was. I reached for my cut-off sweats but I couldn't bring myself to be near anything that reminded me of Dank and the nights he spent singing me to sleep. Instead, I took out my nightgown and slipped it over my head. It was pale pink. I smiled sadly, realizing that I'd never thought of that before. I immediately took it off and let it fall to the floor. I couldn't wear it either. I opened my closet and pulled out a t-shirt I had of Leif's and slipped it on. I could still smell Leif and it gave me a sense of power to be able to snub my noise at Dank and embrace Leif with my actions, even if my heart felt differently. I walked over to my bed and laid down, thinking of the music I wouldn't hear. The silence echoed through the house but I knew I wasn't alone. He was watching. I didn't want to close my eyes, hoping he would come to sit in his chair and play music just for me. The only sound I could hear was the slow drip of the faucet in the bathroom and the settling of the house. Had Dank not been downstairs, each small sound would have had me jumping and running for the door. However, with him watching over me I was able to close my eyes and be softly lulled to sleep by the silence.

Music drifted into my dreams. Hauntingly sweet music filled the hole torn in my heart. I smiled, reaching for the source of the sound but I found nothing. It was only a beautiful dream.

# Chapter Eleven

The next morning Dank was gone. I expected it but I still ran downstairs in case he'd stayed. The days went by and Dank continued to ignore me. During the days at school he continued to flirt with Kendra. I had become invisible where he was concerned. At night he would walk into the living room around bedtime and sit on the couch without acknowledging me. Nothing made sense. No matter how many times I tried to get him to talk to me he remained silent. A person could only suffer a certain amount of humiliation and I'd reached my quota. If he wanted to ignore me then fine. I'd let him.

"I'm not taking no for an answer. If I have to personally come to your house and dress you and then have Wyatt pick you up and haul you over his shoulder to the concert, I will. Do not doubt me." Miranda stood with her hand on her hip and a determined set to her chin. Arguing with her when she was like this was pointless.

Wyatt chuckled. "I'll haul her if I have to but maybe we should discuss the hauling part with Leif first. I'm not real sure he's going to want me throwing his girl over my shoulder."

Miranda waved a hand at him, "Whatever! He won't make her do anything she doesn't want to do. You're going to have to haul her and I'm going to have to tackle Leif and sit on him while you make the get away."

I laughed and it surprised me how good it felt. "What is this about you sitting on me?" Leif asked as he walked up and slid his arm around my waist.

Miranda rolled her eyes. "I am trying to explain to Pagan that I'm not taking NO for an answer. She's going to the concert tonight and that is final."

Leif lightly squeezed my hip. "So we're talking about a possible hostage situation then?" he said in a teasing voice.

Wyatt chuckled. "Apparently so."

Leif gazed down at me, grinning wickedly. "You wanna make a run for it and see if they can keep up?"

I laughed and shook my head. "No, it's okay. I'll go if it is so important to Miranda."

Miranda let out an overly dramatic sigh. "Oh good, I wasn't looking forward to tackling him."

"It would've been hilarious to watch you try." Wyatt chortled and I tried really hard not to think about the fact I'd just agreed to go to the benefit concert Cold Soul was giving down on the beach. Seeing Dank on stage with the same guitar in his hands he'd played for me so many nights and hearing his voice being shared with thousands of people made the hole in my heart throb. If I could figure out a way to fill the aching, I would. Nothing seemed to help.

"It's going to be amazing, Pagan. I know you don't really care for Dank Walker but trust me he can blow." Miranda slipped her arm inside Wyatt's and gazed up at him with a coy grin. "But he can't shoot three pointers like you can, baby, so wipe that frown off your sexy face." Wyatt grinned and kissed the top of her head.

Seeing the love in Miranda's eyes when she looked at Wyatt made the hole in my heart ache even more. I would never love Leif that way. Dank Walker had damaged my heart and claimed it in the process.

"Just so you don't start drooling over the rock star. I'm a fan of his stuff, too, but I can learn to hate him real quick if I feel the need to be jealous." Wyatt's tone sounded teasing but no one doubted what he said was the truth.

Leif chuckled. "I don't think I need to worry about Pagan drooling. Cold Soul doesn't sing her type of music. I have a feeling we won't be there very long."

Miranda glared over at Leif. "Don't give her any ideas or excuses. I'm not kidding. I will attempt to tackle your ass if you even look at the exit the wrong way." Leif threw back his head and laughed.

"I'm really glad you have a good sense of humor," Wyatt said with a grin, "Your arms are much bigger than mine."

I began to laugh but the urge died instantly when my eyes found Dank. He stood in front of Kendra whose back was against the wall while she smiled up at him. He leaned down and whispered in her ear. It took all my strength and self-preservation to tear my eyes away from the intimacy between them. My breaths became shallow from the pain in my chest. Leif must have sensed the change in me because he pulled me closer against his side and caressed my bare arm. The farther we walked away from Dank the easier it became to breathe.

The night gulf breeze was unusually warm considering it was

late fall. A large stage with bright lights surrounding it was set up on the Boardwalk facing the beach. There were thousands of people covering the sandy shore. Bonfires could be seen farther down away from the crowd. A couple of high school students were already getting handcuffed for underage drinking. They wouldn't be the first or the last tonight. I held tightly to Leif's hand as we had to zigzag through the crowd, following in Miranda's wake. She had arranged for her father's company to buy some of the special seating supplied under a large tent for a much higher ticket price. I would have been happy to join the mass numbers on the sand but Miranda wouldn't have it. We stopped at the entrance.

"Miranda Wouters and three guests," she said with a haughty air that only seemed to come out when she was throwing her father's power around. She didn't do it often, unless she wanted something, such as getting us out of speeding tickets. Harold Wouters owned Wouters Realty. Wouters Realty handled all the high-end commercial property in the county. In other words, they owned the town.

"Right this way, Miss. Wouters," the young woman said as she turned and led us up front to a row of seating that gave us a perfect view of the stage.

Great, I wouldn't just have to hear the voice I so desperately missed but I was going to have a perfect view of him too. I glanced over at Leif who raised his eyebrows as if impressed with our seats and gave me one of his eager grins. Faking a headache wasn't going to work. Miranda would flip out and Leif really seemed to be excited about this seating arrangement.

"We are set up! That's what I'm talking about." Wyatt stood, grinning and looking around toward the elaborate refreshment table set up at the end of the tent.

"You boys can eat to your hearts' desire. Go on and stop drooling," Miranda said with a pleased smile on her face.

Wyatt kissed her loudly on the lips and glanced back at Leif. "Come on, man, let's go attack this fancy grub." Leif turned to me as if asking for permission. I nodded. He reminded me of a loyal puppy dog. He bent down and gave me a quick peck on the lips before following Wyatt.

"Stop frowning like I've brought you to a smoke-filled bar. Come on, girl, and enjoy yourself." I forced a smile, which only caused Miranda's frown to deepen. "What happened with you, Pagan? You use to have difficulty not looking at Dank and getting a silly look of adoration on your face. Now, you see him and you look like you're about to throw up. Did he hurt your feelings or something? Is that why you don't want to be here?"

Did he hurt me? She could never know just how badly he'd hurt me. I shook my head and tried even harder to make my smile seem more realistic.

"Of course not. I just realized he was a jerk. Something about him is cold and I don't like being near him." I gazed out at the waves crashing along the shore. If she searched too deeply into my eyes, I was afraid she would see the agony.

"Hmmm, okay then. I guess you're right about the cold thing. Something about him seems hard and so unreal."

She had no idea how unreal he was.

The breeze had started to cool off and the seating under the tent filled to capacity. I wanted to be anywhere other than right here with a perfect view of the stage Dank would soon perform on. The lights dimmed and the crowd went wild. Leif put his arm around my back and I leaned into him, hoping his nearness would help me make it through this. With a drum roll and the sound of an electric guitar the lights flashed brightly as fireworks went off overhead. A group of three guys had taken the stage. One sat behind the drums with long blond dreadlocks and the other two stood on each side of the stage with guitars in their hands. The music filled the night air and screams went out from the beach. The shoreline was so covered in people you could no longer see the sand. A loud bang and a cloud of smoke caused me to jump. The cheering and chanting only got louder. Dank walked out of the smoke now seeping over the stage. I watched as his dark hair danced in the breeze and he reached the microphone waiting in the center of the stage. He took it in his hands and then turned directly toward the tent. Directly toward me.

*"You want what you can't have. I see it in your eyes. The pain that fills your nights is because of my pack of lies. I've opened up the door for you to walk away. There's a better path for you even though I want you to stay. I've broken the rules, I've veered from the path but when I met you I knew to save you was worth the wrath. Let me leave now before it's too late. Let me leave now before you know what I am and your love becomes hate.*

*Walk away from me before I break down and take you with me. You can't go where I'm going you can't walk through my Hell.*

*Walk away from me before I break down and take you with me. My path is meant for only me. There is no way to take you too. I've given you life when it was in my hands to give you death. Walk away from me.*

*I watch the life I know you will lead without me here. It's what you deserve it is where you belong it is everything I want but everything I fear. Once I met you I knew I had to save you but you saved me. Now I'm turning away and letting you run free. Not one moment will I forget there is a fire inside me that you lit with your touch. Hurting you wasn't the plan but it must happen by my hand.*

*Walk away from me before I break down and take you with me. You can't go where I'm going you can't walk through my Hell. Walk away from me before I break down and take you with me. My path is meant for only me. There is no way to take you too. I've given you life when it was in my hands to give you death. Walk away from me."*

My hands trembled in my lap. His gaze never left mine. The words were meant for me. I couldn't manage to breathe past the pain constricting my throat. Why was he doing this? Hadn't he hurt me enough? The tears stinging my eyes would fall free, rolling down my cheeks announcing to my friends how much Dank's words affected me. They couldn't know. No one could. I stood up and walked away. I couldn't sit there and listen anymore. In some sort of desperate trance I pushed past screaming fans and sweaty bodies. I could breathe if I could just get away; put some distance between me and his words. Once I stepped out of the tent, I turned and ran toward the darkness. Away from the fear. I wasn't scared of him but I was scared of his words. He was leaving. My stomach clenched at the thought and I ran harder until the sandy beach was dark and empty. The sound of the music played in the distance and I glanced back over my shoulder to see if Leif or Miranda had managed to follow me. No one was coming. I was truly alone. Gasping for breath I dropped to my knees and let out the sob I'd been fighting to hold in since he began singing. Hot tears trailed down my face. My chest hurt so badly, and deep breaths were impossible.

The night air dropped several degrees. It wasn't my pain stifling my breathing, it was the coldness that came with her. I turned around slowly, knowing she was there watching me. I could feel her presence. She was icy fear. Yet the aching black hole Dank had left in my chest made the danger she possessed pale in comparison. I stood up and faced her, realizing my fear had been replaced with hate. She no longer scared me. She made me angry. Something about her appearance caused Dank distress and it made me want to hurt her for the part she was playing in my pain. I glared at her as the blond hair floated, unhindered by the gulf breeze.

"What is it you want from me?" I yelled through my tears. I took a step toward her, clenching my hands into fists. I didn't want her to think she could make me cower. I didn't want her to think she could frighten me anymore. Her tinkling giggle filled the darkness around us.

"It is appointed," she said in a voice I had grown to abhor.

"What is appointed? Huh? Do you even know? Get a freaking life and leave me the Hell alone!" I stepped closer to her, wanting to take a swing at her but knowing it wouldn't do any good.

Her tinkling laughter turned into a deep sinister laugh. "It was appointed and he broke the rules." Her laughter died and she glared back at me. "You! He broke the rules for you! Why you? What is it about you? A simple human with an appointed time. It was all very simple yet he made it all so difficult." She crooked her finger at me. "Come on, come closer and I'll right his wrong." I swallowed and the fear I thought I'd overcome was slowly returning. Dank had also said she'd come to right a wrong.

"What wrong?" I asked.

She tilted her head as if studying me. "You are different than the others. I suppose that was intriguing to him. His existence is rather monotonous."

I fought back the urge to lunge at her, knowing full well I'd probably go right through her. She wanted me to come closer. I needed to keep my distance. I shook my head and took a step back. In a blur of light she was standing in front of me and my breath began to grow even more shallow. I tried to step back but an icy hand wrapped around my wrist and began pulling me with a force I couldn't fight against toward the crashing waves. The first splash of cold, salty water startled me. This was real. This time I was alone and no one would hear me.

I began kicking and fighting but she continued to drag me out into the gulf with little effort. There was no chance I would survive out in the deep water. The waves were getting taller and she was pulling me under. She was going to drown me. Couldn't she just kill me by suffocating me as she had begun to do at school before Dank had interrupted? The lights and music danced in the distance. This time I was alone and no one would save me. Strangely enough I didn't want to scream. I didn't fear death any longer. But I wish I'd been able to say goodbye.

I closed my eyes as the water reached my chin and the first wave crashed over my head. As I allowed my body to go limp and accept this fate, I heard someone scream my name. Had someone found me out here? I started to jerk away from her grasp and call out but it dawned on me she'd probably just take their life too. She wasn't here for them. I had to go silently. Whoever had come for me didn't deserve this fate.

A bright flash of light filled the dark water and my wrist was immediately released from her icy grip. I fought to find the surface of the water and draw air into my burning lungs.

"*NO!* I said NO! I made this choice and I broke this rule but it was mine to break. I have let your interference go unpunished long enough. This ends now."

I wanted to open my eyes and see him. I could hear him but the salt water stinging my eyes was making it impossible. Another wave crashed over me and I began kicking frantically as water filled my unprepared nose. Warm arms encircled my waist and I clung to them knowing they belonged to him. I was safe now. My head broke the surface and I began to choke on the salt water.

"Here, let me." Dank wiped my eyes with a cool cloth and the stinging disappeared as did my coughing. It was as if I'd never been forced under cold sea waves. Finally I could see Dank's face. He was holding me again.

"Why, Pagan?" He closed his eyes and touched his forehead to mine and took a deep breath. "Why? You knew she was still stalking you. You felt her. Why did you come out here alone? Did you want to find her? Did you think facing her alone was the answer?"

I shook my head and stared up into his eyes so close to mine. "No, I just wanted to get away. I needed to think. Watching you...." I stopped before saying any more.

A sad smile touched his mouth. "All she could do was attempt to kill you. In order for you to truly face death, Death would have had to come and take you. That wasn't going to happen." He stopped and took in a ragged breath before touching his lips to my head. His lips moved to my cheek before lingering over my mouth. "As much as I want to kiss you, I can't." He let out a soft chuckle. "You frustrating girl. You're like no other soul I've ever known." I touched his face and leaned forward to touch my lips to his but he pulled back and shook his head. "No," he whispered, "Don't. I can't. You're too special. My desire for you overpowers what I know is best for you. I can't risk that again."

"Don't leave me," I begged.

He touched my lips with his fingertip. "I won't. At least not tonight."

# Chapter Twelve

"What did you do all weekend? Leif said you hadn't felt well after the concert. I thought I would hear something from you. But I got nothing, nada. Cold Soul was rocking awesome. You should have stayed afterward. We met the band, well except for their lead singer, Dank. He left earlier or something. I didn't care, it was amazing! I could have kissed Daddy's face for that one." Miranda hooked her arm in mine as she babbled on. I scanned the hall, needing to see Dank somewhere in the sea of faces. "Who're you looking for?" There was a touch of interest in Miranda's voice. Dank was nowhere in the crowd, however, Kendra was and she was flirting openly with Justin. That seemed strange.

"Have you seen Dank this morning?" I asked, looking at Miranda and praying she didn't read any more into my question.

Her forehead wrinkled in a frown. "Dank as in Dank Walker, the lead singer of Cold Soul?"

I nodded and scanned the lockers. "Yes, Dank," I repeated. The confused frown on Miranda's face triggered an alarm bell in my head.

"Um, are you taking those pain meds again, sweetie? Why would the lead singer of Cold Soul be here?"

Something was very wrong. Panic swelled in my chest.

"Good morning," Leif said as he walked up to me and slipped his arm around my shoulders.

Miranda glanced up at him with a worried smile. "Morning, Leif. It's so sweet that you go get all her books the minute you two arrive. Would you think of giving Wyatt some pointers?"

"No way." Leif chuckled and squeezed my shoulders gently. Normally having him close helped me when I was on the verge of panic. However, right now I needed to know where Dank was and why Miranda didn't seem to know what I was talking about.

I glanced up at Leif. "Have you seen Dank?" The same confused frown came over his face.

"Who?" he asked, equally confused.

"She asked me the same thing. I'm thinking she might have had to take some pain meds again this morning. Are you still hurting? Does your mom know? 'Cause, girl, you are a trippin' on something if you think that Dank Walker is at our school." Miranda and Leif were both looking at me as if I was a need for concern. I glanced over at Kendra, who was draped around Justin.

"Is Kendra dating Justin now?" I asked in a tone I hoped was conversational and didn't betray the panic raging inside me.

Leif's frown deepened. "They've been dating for months now. Are you okay, Pagan?"

I forced a smile and nodded. "Oh, um, I forgot. No, I'm fine. I just need to make a stop into the restroom before I go to first period." I stood on my tippy toes, kissed Leif quickly on the lips, and headed off the other way. I needed to escape their scrutiny so I could think. Dank was gone and no one remembered him.

The restroom was blessedly empty. I dropped my books down on the damp counter and leaned against the wall for support. My heart contracted so painfully in my chest I feared it might just stop working. Someone came inside and I turned to walk into a stall. I needed privacy for my mental breakdown. But after only two steps it dawned on me the door to the restroom had never opened. I froze, took a deep breath, and then peered back at the other occupant. A dark-haired teenage girl had drifted through the wall. I turned and took a step toward her and she noticed me. She seemed surprised I could see her and a smile broke out on her face.

"Who are you?" I asked, but she only watched me. "Can you talk to me?" I was no longer worried about ignoring them. Maybe they held the answers. She shook her head and her smile turned sad. She drifted closer to me and reached out and touched my hair. Nothing. No shiver or chill. It was as if she wasn't there. This was what I'd always known of souls. "Why can't you speak?" I asked and she moved until she was standing in front of me. She shook her head at me as if correcting me from asking that question. "You aren't allowed to talk to me or you can't?" I wasn't scared of her. I knew she had no power to hurt me. Her frown grew agitated and she shook her head again and backed away from me slowly.

I took a step closer to her. "Please, I need some answers and I think you could help me." Her frown turned fearful and she continued shaking her head and backing away from me as if I were something to be frightened of. "Please," I begged and at my last plea she turned and vanished into the wall.

I stared at the wall until the restroom door opened and a freshman girl walked in. She stopped and studied me. I must have looked like an idiot standing there staring at an empty wall. I smiled at her reassuringly. Maybe this incident wouldn't make it all over school. Not that I cared if people talked about me. I just didn't need Miranda and Leif worrying over me anymore. Besides, I needed answers and I was so tired of waiting around for Dank to tell me. The young soul hadn't been able to help me for reasons I couldn't understand. However, I had a feeling that if I kept searching I would soon find one who was ready to talk or could talk.

The hallways were already empty which meant I was late for English Literature. The ache returned as I thought about facing class without Dank. Even when he'd been ignoring me I was able to hear him talk and feel the heat from his gaze. Now, I wasn't even going to have that small bit of comfort. What hurt even worse was how no one seemed to remember him. It was as if he had never existed. I stopped right outside the door. Going inside seemed unbearable. I wrapped my hands around my stomach to hold in the pain tearing me apart and leaned up against the wall. I stared down the empty hallway, wishing another soul would wander through. Instead, the empty silence remained. For the first time in my life I wanted to be bothered by the presence of souls and there wasn't one around. If I could just go somewhere that was infested with wandering souls then I could ask them all. I could ask and ask until I found one could and would speak to me. Something about the young soul in the bathroom told me she could have spoken had she wanted. She was scared. Scared of what? What did souls have to fear? They were dead after all, or at least their bodies were.

"The hospital," I whispered aloud, remembering that the one place I'd seen endless wandering souls had been the hospital. I turned and headed toward the front doors to the school. I would go there and start asking every soul I found. One of them was bound to talk back. I would figure out how to find Dank. He was real. I'd known him. I loved him. I would find him.

"Miss. Moore? Our class is this way," Mr. Brown's voice cut through my thoughts and I stopped and sighed in defeat before turning around and facing my round English Literature teacher.

"Yes, sir, I was, um, just going to get a late pass." He smiled and shook his head, "No need, but do hurry up please we're just getting started on the beauty that is fiction. Come along now." He stepped back, waiting for me to enter first. I walked back toward the class, wanting to turn and take off running in the other direction. I knew if Mom got a call that I'd jumped ship she would be furious and my chances of finding Dank were slim to none once I was locked in my room for the rest of the year.

I stepped into the classroom and walked over to my empty seat by the window. The chair behind me sat empty. I glanced back at Kendra and the chair behind her was full of Justin. He'd just stepped in and taken Dank's place. Disgusted, I turned back around. How could she have been touched by Dank and kissed by him and so easily forgotten he existed? I hadn't forgotten. How had she? How could she not feel the pain of his absence? He was too good for her. Why had he wasted so much time with her? I sank down into my chair and swallowed the lump of emotion welling up inside me. I couldn't sit through this class without him here.

"The reading assignment today is to be done quietly at our desks. Do not talk to your neighbors. I want complete silence as you inhale the beauty of the written word. Take it in. Let it soak into your veins and fill you with such glorious wonder that you are positively glow-ing." Moans erupted over the room. "Tsk, tsk, tsk. Let us be excited about the word. Excited about its beauty." Grumbling continued as the sounds of shuffling pages filled the room. This would be a time for most of the students to take a nap behind their textbooks. I opened mine, wanting to find something to get my thoughts off of Dank. When the day was over I would go to the hospital and I would begin asking questions. Some soul somewhere had answers.

"Ugh, this is poet stuff," a grumbling voice came from the back of the room.

Mr. Brown looked up from the book in his hands. "Ah, yes it is Mr. Kimbler, so nice of you to notice." More groans erupted and I found the page directed on the board. It was William Wordsworth's work. I felt the urge to moan in despair myself. Studying the begin-ning of the Romantic Age was not something I needed right now. Where were the tragic playwrights when you needed them?

"How does this mess help us in the real world?" Justin said in a cocky voice. Sniggers erupted across the classroom.

"Hear, hear," someone called with a tap on their desk.

Mr. Brown glanced up once more with a slightly annoyed ex-pression on his face, "Gentlemen, if one does not study the words of famous romantic poets how will one ever learn to woo the woman they will one day love? I can assure you that P Diddy has no words of instruction in his lyrical creations." His words caused a few chuckles. I would have found this all very amusing if the concept of reading P Diddy lyrics didn't seem so appealing at the moment. I glanced down at the poem we were to read and write a two-page paper on. *To a Young Lady* by William Wordsworth. I could only hope it wasn't a poem of enduring love.

*"Dear Child of Nature, let them rail!*
*--There is a nest in a green dale,*
*A harbour and a hold,*
*Where thou a Wife and Friend, shalt see*
*Thy own delightful days, and be*
*A light to young and old.*
*There, healthy as a Shepherd-boy,*
*As if thy heritage were joy,*
*And pleasure were thy trade,*
*Thou, while thy Babes around thee cling,*
*Shalt shew us how divine a thing*
*A Woman may be made.*

*Thy thoughts and feelings shall not die,*
*Nor leave thee, when grey hairs are nigh,*
*A melancholy slave*
*But an old age, alive and bright,*
*And lovely as a Lapland night,*
*Shall lead thee to thy grave.*
*"--_Pleasure is spread through the earth*
*In stray gifts to be claim'd by whoever shall find_."*

My shattered heart throbbed. I began to write. The pain inside me poured out onto the paper. It felt almost as if I were bleeding with each word I scrawled. Lost in my need to express to someone the pain inside, it startled me when my paper was taken from under my hand. My head snapped up. Mr. Brown gave me a small nod and cleared his throat.

"Ah, it appears that Miss. Moore knows William Wordsworth or has already read her homework." He peered over his half-moon spectacles at the class. "Which is much more than I can say about the lot of you." He stared back down at my paper and straightened his short, round structure.

"Wordsworth was remembering his sister whom he'd been re-proached for taking long walks with in the country. He was thinking of her life and the fullness she would experience. He congratulated her or praised her in her efforts to enjoy the beauty around her rather than follow the rules."

The bell rang and students began scrambling to get out of the classroom for fear Mr. Brown was going to force them to listen to more of my paper, or worse, snatch theirs up to read aloud. He laid my paper back down on my desk and smiled at me. "You are truly a delight, Pagan. I look forward to reading the rest of this in the morning." He turned and headed back to his desk with a waddle.

Leif walked into the classroom grinning at me. "You coming, gorgeous? I know you like English Literature but it's over for the day."

Mr. Brown beamed at me. "Ah, yes, but anytime you want to stop in to discuss its beauty, please feel free."

"Thank you, Mr. Brown." That wouldn't be happening but he really was a sweet, old man. A tad eccentric, but sweet.

"Don't give her any ideas, Mr. Brown," Leif teased as he took the books from my hands.

"Ah, the handsome man who owns her heart does not want to share," Mr. Brown said with a grin that pushed his thick cheeks back only slightly.

Leif chuckled. "You're correct."


"Now, tell me again what it is that you're going to do that's more important than shopping for the perfect winter boots?" Miranda's right hand perched on her hip as she gaped at me as if I'd just spoken Spanish. I slipped my book bag up higher on my shoulder and kept my eyes on the parking lot.

"I'm going to go sign up for volunteer work at the hospital." I didn't have a real moral explanation for this. I couldn't bring myself to tell Miranda how I felt the need to give of myself or whatever one would say that feels the need to go volunteer to help the sick and dying. The truth was I hated hospitals and Miranda knew this. She didn't know why I hated them. She just knew I did. I'd never been able to explain to her how the wandering souls who filled the halls of the hospitals bothered me.

"So, you're over the hospital dislike thingy now that you've spent a week in there?" she asked curiously. I shrugged because my stay had nothing to do with it.

"Guess so." It was as good an excuse as any.

"Alright then, if you must go do something for the greater good of others while I go do something for the greater good of my winter wardrobe then I guess I'm good with that."

I flashed her a smile and then headed toward Leif's car. He'd left me his keys and said he would get a ride home with Justin. I'd fed him this "I want to go volunteer" stuff too. It wasn't a total lie. I'd decided this was the best way to see enough souls without someone admitting me into the crazy ward for wandering the halls talking to myself.  This way I had a reason to be there and I would find plenty of souls to speak to. Eventually, I would come across one that spoke.

"Call me when you get home from your good deeds and I'll bring over my purchases and show you."

"Okay, good luck," I called as I unlocked the car door and slipped inside. For the first time in three days I had some hope.  I kept remembering the look in Dank's eyes Friday night as he held me.  He'd been very real. The fact that no one seemed to think he'd ever walked the halls of our school didn't mean I was going crazy. The fact was I had been seeing people no one else could see since birth. Something was different about me. This wasn't break-ing news.  Dank had secrets and I was going to crack them. I needed to know because I needed him. The answer behind his leaving lay within his secrets and I knew if I could figure it out then I could find him and bring him back.

# Chapter Thirteen

I glanced down at my ID tag. My mother would be thrilled. This was going to look wonderful on my college applications. The more community service the better, well, as long as it's voluntary and not mandatory. I'd been assigned the duty of reading to the children today since it was my first day and they didn't have anyone to train me to do the more difficult jobs.

I stepped off the elevator at the pediatric floor and three of the souls I'd passed on the previous floor stood watching me. I nodded to them. "Hello," I said brightly and they all seemed surprised. I turned and followed the directions the front desk volunteer had given me. It didn't take me but a few moments to realize the pediatric floor was full of wandering souls. I walked past kids in wheelchairs watching me with curiosity. I smiled and said hello as I passed by them. My heart began to ache for reasons other than my loss. Seeing the little smiles on their pale faces wasn't easy. A little girl with long, red, curly hair caught my attention. She stood at the door to her hospital room staring, not at me but on either side of me and behind me with curiosity before looking directly at me. I slowed my walk and glanced back, realizing that most of the souls I had smiled at and spoken to were following me. She could see them. I stopped and studied her little, sweet face. She was standing up with the use of what appeared to be a walker. She glanced back at them again and smiled warmly and then her little eyes found me. "Do you see them?" I asked in a whisper, afraid others would hear me and think I was insane. She nodded sending her head of red curls bouncing around her.

"Do you?" she asked me in a loud whisper. I nodded. "Cool," she replied, grinning. I winked and then continued on my way to the activity room. I couldn't stand and talk to a child in the halls about the souls we could both see without drawing attention. I'd never met anyone else who could see souls. It was hard to just walk away from her knowing little face. But I knew I would see her again. I intended to find her later.

I found the sky blue door with the quote, *"Today you are You, that is truer than true. There is no one alive who is Youer than You." - Dr. Seuss*, painted on it in bright colors. This was where I was supposed to be. I opened it up and immediately found the shelves of books to the right.

I turned back and smiled at the souls who'd followed me inside, "Do any of you have a suggestion?" They all studied me and some drew closer to watch me or touch me. I couldn't feel them. "No one?" The room remained silent. I sighed and turned back to the books. "Very well, I'll pick one out myself."

"My favorite is Where the Wild Things Are." I spun back around thinking a soul had finally spoken. The souls were all watching the little red headed girl from the hallway. She was standing at the open door smiling at me. "They won't talk to you, you know. They can't," she said as she walked inside.

"They can't?" I asked staring down into her eyes that appeared so much older than her little body.

She shook her head sadly and sighed. "No, I've tried to get them to. They like for you to talk to them." She paused. "Well, some of them like for you to talk to them but they can't talk back. They are souls fighting their return so they stay here and wander aimlessly." She glanced back over her shoulder at them with a sigh. "But they start to forget who they are or why they are here. It's sad, really. If they would have gone on in the first place then their souls would have been given another body and another life instead of this pointless existence."

I walked over and sat down on the chair in front of her. "How do you know this?" I asked, amazed someone so small could know so much more than me about the souls I'd seen my whole life.

She shrugged. "I guess he didn't want me to be scared. They are scared of him, you see, and he didn't want me to be scared of him. He didn't want me to be scared of them either. And I think maybe he didn't want me to become like them."

I shook my head trying to figure out who she was talking about. "What do you mean? Who is he?"

She frowned and the souls who had gathered in the room vanished. "They're scared of him, like I said. He's the only thing they do remember because he was the last thing they saw while alive. Silly, really, it isn't his fault. It was just their appointed time." I froze at her words and grabbed the arm of the chair I was sitting in for support.

My heart started pounding in my chest as I asked, "What do you mean by 'appointed time'?"

She studied me a minute and then whispered, "It was their appointed time to die. Just like mine will come soon. He told me. He wasn't supposed to but he can break the rules if he wants. No one can stop him. It's ultimately his decision." I swallowed the bile in my throat at the mention of this little girl talking about her death.

"Who told you?" I asked again.

She shook her head. "Don't look so sad. He said this body I have is sick and once I die I'll get a new body and a new life. Souls aren't forced to wander the Earth. Only those too scared to go on are left here to wander. If you chose to leave the Earth you'll return in a new body and a new life. Your soul will, however, be the same. He told me the man who wrote my favorite books, *The Chronicles of Narnia,* said that 'You are not a body. You have a body. You are a Soul'." She smiled at the idea like it was brilliant.

I took a deep breath to calm myself before asking one more time. "Who is 'he'?"

She frowned. "The author? C.S. Lewis."

I shook my head. "No, the 'he' that has told you all of this. The 'he' that the souls are scared of." She frowned and turned around to leave. "No, wait, please...I need to know who he is," I begged.

She glanced back at me and shook her head. "Until it's your appointed time you can't know." She left.

I held the book, *Where the Wild Things Are,* in my hands, ready to read as the kids filed in, but she didn't come with them. I forced a smile and cheerful tone as I read the words I remembered from my childhood. Several kids requested other books when I finished and numbly I got each book off the shelf and read them their request until the nurses insisted it was time to return to their rooms for dinner. After several hugs and 'thank you's I headed back down the halls. This time I didn't bother to smile at the wandering souls. They couldn't help me. I was pretty sure the only one who could was the little girl who'd spoken to 'him' and deep down I feared I knew exactly who 'he' was and what it was he did.

"I have a surprise for you," Leif announced as he sauntered into my living room at seven that night. I peered up from the textbook lying open on the table and smiled at him. Seeing Leif helped ease the hollowness inside me. He bent down, kissed me on the lips softly, and then laid a brochure down in front of me on the table.

"Gatlinburg, Tennessee?" I asked, reading the brochure in front of me with the image of a snowy mountaintop with a ski lift and festively-lit streets.

He beamed and sat down in the chair beside me. "A whole weekend of skiing and shopping. My grandparents have a cabin up there we go to this time every year. I spoke with Miranda and she has got the go-ahead from her dad. He's covering the cost of travel and spending for her and Wyatt, and my parents want to treat you in return for all your hard work in helping me achieve an A in Speech." He grinned wickedly. "And because they knew I wouldn't go unless you did."

Going on a skiing holiday wasn't something I wanted to think about right now. Emotionally, I was barely hanging on and I needed to find Dank. I just couldn't figure out how I was going to find him exactly.

"Wow." I forced a smile. He took my fake smile as encouragement and opened the brochure. He began talking about all the things to do on top of the mountain. I was trying to wrap my mind around how I could tell him no when my mother walked in.

"Hello, Leif, have you eaten yet? I brought home Chinese from the meeting with my literary agent. Are either of you hungry?" she asked.

"I'm starved," Leif said with enthusiasm.

"No, thanks," I replied. The thought of food turned my stomach. I realized Leif was telling my mother about the ski trip and I panicked, trying to think of some way to stop this.

"Oh, that would be perfect, Pagan. Aunt Margie has asked us to come to the ranch for Thanksgiving but I hated to take you back there to witness her mourn her first Thanksgiving without Ted. She needs me and I could go if you were spending the holiday in the mountains with friends. I won't feel like you're suffering at all. That is just perfect. Leif, thank you. I need to call your parents tonight and get details. I want to send money with her, though, I don't like the idea of your parents paying for her."

Leif shook his head. "Oh, no, ma'am, that's not necessary. They want to pay for her. She has been an answer to their prayers with my Speech grade this year. They couldn't have paid for a better tutor." He flashed a wicked grin down at me and then smiled politely back at my mom.

They were planning this as if it was a done deal. Mom wasn't going to tell me no or question it. I had no way out unless I wanted to hurt not only Leif, who didn't deserve it, but Miranda too. She was no doubt thrilled about the trip and even though all I wanted to do was search for Dank, I couldn't. At the moment I wasn't sure how to begin to look for Dank. My plan had come to a crumbing halt. In a sudden burst of hope I'd checked Ebay for Cold Soul tickets thinking maybe if I went to a concert I could see him and know he was real. I could wipe out all these fears stirring inside of me that he was something I couldn't have or touch. Even if I could afford the tickets I couldn't afford the travel cost to get to his upcoming concert dates.

"I guess that's what we need to do tomorrow," Mom said brightly. I had no idea what she was talking about.

I stared up at her and frowned. "What?"

She rolled her eyes. "Go buy your snow gear, silly. You're going to need heavier winter clothing as well. Oh, this is going to be so much fun! I'm so excited about this. You two do your homework and I'm going to call Margie and let her know I'll be there Thanksgiving." Mom left us and Leif turned back around, smiling triumphantly, a box of fried rice in one hand and chopsticks in the other.

"She is cooler than cool, I swear. Wyatt's parents put up a little fight. She was so easy." He kissed the top of my head as he walked back around to sit down at the table. "You better call Miranda and tell her the good news before we get started. She's waiting to hear from you." I nodded and reached for my phone. I was going to have to act excited for Leif's sake, and hers. The phone rang once before intense squealing erupted on the other line.

"Please say she said yes, please, please, please," Miranda's voice sang on the other line.

"She said yes," I replied with a smile in Leif's direction.

"FANTABULOUS! We're going to have such a good time. Shopping in the snow. How romantic is that? I mean really does it get any better than snow on quaint little streets full of shops? No, it doesn't. However, I'll warn you now, I'm not putting my foot in a ski. No way. I want to shop, not visit the ER for a big 'ole ugly cast. Are you going to ski?" I glanced at Leif who could obviously hear her voice over the phone. He was nodding with a big grin on his face.

"I don't know that I have a choice in the matter." I replied.

"Ugh, well, I do and I'm not doing it. I mean, you fall and get cold wet bottoms. No way. Not going to do it."

Leif chuckled. "You wear a snow suit, Miranda, it keeps your bottom dry," he called out loudly.

"Whatever, still not doing it. Oh, I need to call Wyatt and tell him. We have got to go shopping for real winter clothes. You'll have to put your community service aside for one afternoon or possibly two. Okay, well! SQUEEAAAA! I'll talk to you later." She hung up.

I closed my phone and laid it down on the table. "She may be a little hard to live with the next two weeks," I said jokingly.

Leif nodded. "I think you may be right." He leaned back in his chair. "So, tell me about this community service." I didn't want to talk to him about this. I stared down at the notebook in front of me.

"Well, I'm working as a volunteer at the hospital. Today I read books to kids." I hoped that was all the information he needed. I peered up at him and the admiration in his eyes made me feel like a terrible person. I hadn't gone to volunteer because I was concerned about others. I'd gone to find answers. However, I'd found all the answers I was likely to get there. She had just been a kid, but she had spoken like she knew exactly what she was talking about. Tomorrow I thought about talking to the elderly I knew didn't have much time left to see if any of them would tell me if they had seen this "he" she referred to.

"You're one special girl, Pagan Moore, and I'm incredibly lucky," Leif said, gazing at me with an emotion in his eyes I didn't deserve.

I shook my head. "No, I'm as normal as they come. Trust me. Now, let's get some homework done." I needed to change the subject before I broke down in tears and admitted what a horrible person I really was. I used Leif as a comfort and I had for so long. Now, I was using sick people to help me find Dank. Would I stop at nothing to find him? Was love meant to be this intense?

"Okay, this week we are faced with the challenging question: Should high school students rely on the aid of coffee in the mornings? Real deep, huh?" I managed a laugh I didn't feel and reached for my laptop.

"I think we need to google this one. Because I for one think coffee is the nectar of the gods and, yes, we need it desperately. However, I'm thinking your teacher thinks differently."

Leif shrugged. "I hate the stuff so I'm no help. Do you really think the internet is going to have information on this?"

I glanced over at him as I clicked enter. "Um, yes I do. We will have the health conscious groups' arguments and Starbucks arguments both at our fingertips in just a second."

Existence

Leif leaned over, peered at the screen, and grinned. "Cool, so which side do I take for this speech?"

# Chapter Fourteen

The streets were already decorated with twinkling, white Christmas lights on every tree. Shop windows were decked out with holiday cheer. The streets smelled of warm fudge and mountain taffy from the candy shops littered around every corner. Snow was drifting down lazily and sticking to our coats as we walked the streets. Wyatt held five shopping bags already in his hands, full of Miranda's purchases. An icy breeze made my numb nose throb. I ducked down into the scarf I'd wrapped around the bottom part of my face several times. I was not accustomed to this weather. Our winters in Florida never got this cold. Leif pulled me close to his side. "Come on, let's go into this coffee shop and get something to warm us up."

"Good idea. I need a break from these bags and I'm pretty sure Miranda won't find anything in there to buy." I laughed at Wyatt through the scarf covering my mouth.

I reached up and pulled it down, glancing up at him. "You've got to be kidding. You know she can find something in any store we step inside. So far we've been in five stores and you are holding five bags."

"Pish posh," Miranda said with a wave of her furry gloved hand. "What are all these cute little stores for but to buy things?" Leif chuckled behind me and we all went over to a table. I sighed as the warmth of the coffee house seemed to thaw out my frozen nose. It was the only body part I hadn't been able to cover up.

"What do you want?" Leif asked, taking off his scarf and hanging it and his large black down coat on the chair beside me.

"Caramel latte with whipped cream," I replied. He turned and joined Wyatt at the counter and I glanced over at Miranda.

"My nose feels as if it may fall off from frost bite," I grumbled and rubbed it with my gloved hands.

She nodded and rubbed hers as well. "I know what you mean.

Now that I'm inside and not focused on the shopping, I feel the numbness."

I started to say something else when I noticed the soul standing at the counter watching people order with a confused expression. Now I knew what they were and why they always looked so lost and confused, and I wished I could do something to help them. They could have lived more lives if they'd only moved on. Instead, fear had held them back and all they could hope for was to wander, lost.

"Who are you looking at as if you want to cry?" Miranda asked, poking her chin out over the scarf wrapped around her neck.

I jerked my gaze away from the soul and stared back at her, "No one, I was just lost in thought." Miranda glanced back over her shoulder but all she saw were Wyatt and Leif walking back toward us, holding steaming cups of coffee. Well, at least everyone's but Leif's, his would be hot chocolate.

"Here we go. Let's see if we can get the frozen blood in our veins moving again," Wyatt said jovially as he put Miranda's latte down in front of her. I took mine from Leif and took a small sip, needing to have some warmth flow through me. Miranda took her mug and held it to her nose. I giggled and Wyatt rolled his eyes.

"Laugh all you want but it feels good." I studied my cup and decided I didn't care how silly she looked, I wanted to warm my nose too. The cup's heat felt wonderful to my nose.

"You Florida girls sure have a hard time with a little cold weather."

Miranda lowered her cup and stared at Leif incredulously. "A little cold? Are you crazy? It's like thirty below out there!" She whined and held the cup back up to her nose.

"Um, no. Actually, it's only twenty degrees out there. Not even close to being below zero."

I put my cup back down on the table. "Um, that's like ten degrees below freezing so I'd say it's much colder than a little cold." Miranda smiled at me for coming to her defense and shot Leif a smug smile. Leif's arm slipped around me and I let myself pretend for now that my life was normal: that I loved Leif and my heart wasn't damaged beyond repair because I was in love with someone I couldn't find and feared I never would again. My best friend's tinkling laughter and her happiness to be surrounded by friends and shopping seemed so normal. I could pretend I was whole. I could pretend I was happy and I could pretend a lost soul hadn't just wandered through the wall behind Wyatt searching through the people around him for someone who might have the answer to his problem. No one could help him now. My fake smile was harder to hold in place, but I did because ignoring the supernatural around me was what I'd been doing my entire life.

"I'm thinking we shouldn't be going out tonight. I mean, I know it's not exactly ideal to hang out in a cabin with your parents, Leif, but it's icy out there." Miranda was frowning as she looked outside the window on her side of the Hummer that Leif's parents had rented for us to use while we were here.

"We're inside a monster, baby, no worries." Wyatt leaned over and kissed Miranda's neck, making her giggle. I gazed back toward the road in front of me and away from the happy couple in the back.

"Wyatt's right, Miranda. My parents rented this vehicle so we could get around easily in the icy weather. Besides, the Pancake House is not something you want to miss. Piles of pancakes covered in any topping you can imagine. I'm drooling just thinking about it," Leif replied, grinning.

"UGH! I'm going to be like a thousand pounds when we leave here. All we do is eat. If you make me stop at one more of those mountain taffy stores I think I might run screaming the other way." Miranda pouted in the back seat.

Wyatt laughed. "Or you'll go taste test every sample they have."

Miranda teasingly punched his arm. "Oh hush. Don't remind me of my weakness and the damage I've done to my hips."

"I like your hips just fine." Wyatt replied in a low husky whisper we could clearly hear up front.

"Okay, you two, I'm going to make you walk to the restaurant if you don't cool off back there," Leif warned, flashing them a smile in the rearview mirror.

I kept my attention on the road as the falling snow seemed to get heavier. I touched my seat belt and a small stab of pain pierced me as I remembered Dank standing in my hospital room telling me my seat belt had saved my life. Yet, my mom had said I'd been thrown out for not wearing my seat belt and *not* wearing it had saved my life. I would have been crushed had I been left inside the car. The memory of a heavy weight being on my chest making it hard for me to breathe hit me. I'd been in the car when it'd finally stopped rolling. I'd thought I would suffocate from the heaviness on me. Then I'd been taken from the car and laid down on the grass. The pain had been so intense I couldn't open my eyes. How had I gotten out of the car? Someone had gotten me out. Someone had unbuckled my seat belt and lifted me out of the crushed car and laid me safely on the grass. I'd never asked him about the seat belt again.

Now, as I rode along the icy mountain roads it slowly dawned on me. The someone who'd taken me from the accident had to have been the only person who knew I'd been wearing my seat belt. Why had I not asked him again? I'd forgotten about his knowledge I'd been wearing my seat belt. Leif had shown up and I'd let myself forget the wreck and the events leading up to it.

"You okay?" Leif's hand slid across my leg and took my hand in his.

I masked my pain and turned to give him a reassuring smile. "Yes."

He nodded toward the snowy evergreens outside my window. "It's beautiful, isn't it?" I nodded because he was right, it was, but also because it gave me an excuse to keep staring off into the darkness.

"LEIF! WATCH OUT!" Wyatt's voice broke into the soothing quietness of the Hummer like a bullet and Leif jerked the vehicle off the road and skidded up against the side of the mountain before coming to a full stop only feet away from the car that had just hit a patch of ice and flipped right in front of us.

Leif jerked open his door. "Call 911!" he yelled back at us and Wyatt jumped out of the vehicle with him. I reached blindly for my purse, not wanting to take my eyes off the smoking car in case I saw them. The souls who would walk away from it, if the crash had killed the passengers. I'd know soon if they'd died...wouldn't I?

"There has been a really bad wreck in front of us." Miranda's voice came from behind me and I knew she'd found her phone and already made the call. I dropped my purse and crawled over to Leif's seat to get out of his door, since my side was jammed up against the mountain. Sparks started flying from the upturned car and Wyatt grabbed Leif's arm and pulled him back.

"No man, stop," he said and Leif appeared torn as to whether he should try to help them or back away. Sparks and smoke so close to gasoline meant at any moment the car would catch on fire and possibly blow up.

"BACK UP!" Miranda yelled, jumping out of the car and running toward us with the phone in her hand.

"The lady on the phone says to back away. The smoke and sparks are a bad sign and she said the paramedics and fire trucks are on their way but they don't need more injuries to deal with, it won't help the people in the car."

"She's right, Leif, come on. Back up." Leif glanced frantically back at me.

"Move back, Pagan," he called. Before anyone could react, the fire ignited and the car in front of us went up in flames. A scream echoed in my ears and I cringed at the thought of the people inside we hadn't been able to help. Frozen in horror, we all stood there and watched, unable to do anything to save them. Miranda's wails were muffled by Wyatt's soothing voice. Leif's arms came around me and pulled me back farther from the heat of the flames. I let him pull me away but I didn't take my eyes off the car. I needed to see if they were dead.

"Don't watch, Pagan," Leif's voice was in my ear softly pleading. He didn't understand why I had to watch and I couldn't tell him.

Then I saw him. He stepped out of the darkness and walked directly into the fire. I broke free of Leif's hold and ran toward the fire. He was here. Dank was here.

"Pagan, NO!" Leif's voice called from behind me.

"STOP HER!" Miranda called out in a panicked voice, but I couldn't stop. Dank was here! He was in there. The fire wouldn't hurt him. I understood now. Arms wrapped around me and pulled me back as I fought against them.

"*No*, stop, I can't — I need to get there! I need to see," I begged as I struggled against Leif's arms while never taking my eyes off the burning car. Dank emerged with two people by his side. It was a young couple. I started to call out his name as Leif held me tightly

119

in his arms, unyielding.

"Please, please let me go. I need to go," I begged, watching as Dank stopped and stared back at me. His eyes were a glowing, brilliant blue in the darkness as he watched me struggle and call out to him from Leif's arms. He was there, so close, and the people beside him stood staring back at the burning car they had just escaped. He turned from me and with a wave of his hand all three of them were gone. I watched in horror as the darkness returned. The car continued to burn and I heard fire trucks drawing closer.

"Come on, Pagan, come back, baby," Leif whispered in my ear.

"They're dead," I whispered, knowing why Dank had come.

Leif pulled me against him and held me in a tight hug. I let him. He had no idea what I'd just seen. No one did. All they saw was the burning vehicle. I had just seen the beautiful soul who had stolen my heart emerge from the darkness and take the souls of the people inside the burning car. He wasn't a normal soul. He'd always told me he was different. I understood now what he meant. He was different. His existence was cold and lonely. A sob wracked my body and I crumpled against Leif's body. I wept at the realization that Dank was never given a chance to love. He lived within the sadness. He had to walk hand and hand with death. I heard Leif's voice attempting to comfort me but I couldn't accept his words. Nothing he said made any of this okay. Dank wasn't given a chance at life and happiness. My breathing came in gasps from the pain shooting through my heart. It was all too much. I had a limit and I was positive I'd just reached it.

"No, sir, she isn't hurt. We weren't close enough to the car and we all were wearing our seatbelts when I ran the Hummer into the mountain. She isn't handling what we just witnessed well...." Leif's voice trailed off.

An unfamiliar voice spoke from behind me. "She needs to be taken in and given some meds to calm her down. That kind of emotional trauma can leave devastating effects." I tightened my hold on Leif. I couldn't go to the hospital now. I didn't want to see more sickness or lost souls. I shook my head violently against his chest.

"She's terrified and I can't just let her go without me. I can't leave her." I heard Leif argue.

"You can ride with her but she needs some medical attention. This is not a normal way of dealing with something like this. The other girl is handling it well. This one seems to be losing it."

"Okay, but I'm not letting go of her." Leif said with finality to his voice.

"I don't want to go to a hospital," I said, panicked. I pushed away from Leif, trying to get away so I could run to someone safe; someone who wouldn't make me go. No one understood what I would see there. What I'd seen tonight.

"No, don't," I heard Leif protest and I thought for a moment he was talking to me when I felt the prick of a needle and the world went hazy before it faded to black.


"No, they gave her a shot to knock her out. I tried to stop them but it happened before I could do anything." I heard Leif's voice in the darkness.

"I've called her mother and she's terribly worried. I told her not to come. I'm having us flown out of here in a few hours." Mrs. Montgomery's voice sounded concerned.

"How are Miranda and Wyatt?" Leif asked before fingers gently caressed my arms. I knew it was his touch.

"Both are doing fine. Miranda's fine. She's very worried about Pagan. I reassured her Pagan was just resting." There were a few minutes of silence. I let the caressing touch from Leif comfort me. It helped fight the horror I was only barely containing. I knew there was pain waiting for me but I wasn't ready to face it.

"Honey, is she always this unstable? I realize it was a horrible thing to witness, but for her to completely fall apart like this, well, do you think she has some mental issues you might be unaware of?" Leif didn't say anything at first and I wondered if he'd shook his head or shrugged.

I heard him sigh. "I don't know, Mom," he said quietly. Leif always seemed completely blind to my problems. I'd always wondered if he'd just not noticed the way I'd stare and watch things he couldn't see. Then there were my major mood swings he always seemed to overlook. Maybe he'd seen more than I realized. A swell of panic tightened my chest as I realized that I may be losing Leif too. This time he wouldn't be able to ignore my serious issues. I wasn't normal. I never had been.

"You may need to really think about your relationship with her. It isn't healthy to get involved with someone who is this emotionally vulnerable. People this weak emotionally can be dangerous." Leif's hand stopped caressing my arm.

"I didn't ask your opinion. Don't say things like that about Pagan ever again. Do you understand me? Nothing is wrong with her that is dangerous or harmful. She just feels deeper than others."

I thought of how deeply I loved Dank and I couldn't argue with him. I did feel more deeply than was normal.

"I'm sorry, honey. I shouldn't have said anything but this is just concerning for a mother, that's all. I want what is best for you. Make sure she is."

I wanted to open my eyes and say 'Listen to your mother. I'm not good for you Leif,' but I didn't. Because I was selfish and scared.

# Chapter Fifteen

I wasn't sure how long I'd been back home. Time kind of seemed to roll on continuously. No night or day. Getting out of bed seemed almost impossible at times. In my dreams, Dank was there. I just wanted to sleep. Talking was something I just wasn't ready for.

I'd seen the questions and concern in Leif's eyes on the flight home but I hadn't spoken to him. I hadn't wanted to face him now that he knew I had issues, even if he didn't really know what they were. He thought I was crazy and that wasn't my problem at all. My problem was I loved someone I couldn't have. I saw souls who wandered the Earth lost and I'd been attacked by a soul who was intent on killing me. I was the only person who remembered Dank Walker had gone to our school and if I brought up his name again everyone would really think I'd lost my mind. So, yes, I had issues, but not psychiatric ones. I had supernatural ones.

A knock on my bedroom door startled me and I turned to stare at the closed door, knowing it was my mother. My very worried mother. How could I explain to her I was hurting so deeply I wasn't sure I would ever be able to recover? There was a loss in my life like nothing I'd ever known.

"Come in." My voice sounded hoarse from lack of use. My mother opened the door slowly and stuck her head inside as if to take in the atmosphere before walking all the way in.

"You not up to going to school this morning?" she asked with a smile that didn't meet her eyes.

I'd forgotten what day it was but I knew I wasn't ready to face school. I wasn't ready to face Leif or Miranda or Wyatt. I needed to remain in my room and find the strength inside me to keep living. I shook my head and she gave up the pretense of smiling, a worried frown creasing her forehead.

"Honey, you've missed a week of school so far. I have let you stay in here hoping you would overcome the trauma you've experienced. But now I'm getting worried you aren't going to pull out of this. I've been studying your symptoms on the internet and you have all the signs of Post Traumatic Stress Disorder. You're having horrible nightmares and screaming out in your sleep, yelling for dank or sank or crank—I can't understand it through the sobs. You won't leave your room and you aren't taking calls or visitors. When

I try to talk to you it's like you black out on me. You aren't listening to me."

I sat there listening to her. I was suffering from having my heart shattered, broken beyond repair, but I wasn't going to tell her that. I just stayed silent. She seemed to take my silence as encouragement. "I've made a few calls and I got you an appointment with a psychiatrist. I need you to go talk to her. She's really good and works with teenagers solely. She comes very highly recommended and we don't have to tell anyone you're going to see her." Tears sprang into my mother's eyes. She swiped at them and let out a ragged breath. "I... the truth is, I should have sent you years ago. When you were little you would talk about the people in the walls. I thought it was your imagination but now I wonder if somehow you have some unbalanced chemicals and this trauma you've experienced has triggered something." She sniffed. "You talk to yourself at night in here. I hear you speaking to someone. Honey, you need some help."

I nodded. I knew it would ease her fear. She was so worried and I couldn't explain any of this to her without her truly thinking I was insane.

She smiled through her tears and nodded. "Okay good. I'll give you some time but you need to get up and get a shower. Then get dressed and we will ride over to see Doctor Hockensmith. She's expecting us today."

I nodded again and watched as my mother left the room, leaving the door open as a reminder I needed to get up. I had just agreed to go see a psychiatrist. My mother was wasting her money but I knew I had to go or *she* was going to need to see a psychiatrist from the stress I was putting on her emotionally. I hated that I was upsetting her but I couldn't seem to see a way out of the despair consuming me.

The large, two-story, white stucco house stood on stilts facing out over the Gulf of Mexico. My mom slowed down and stared up at the house large enough to hold at least five families comfortably. But then, it wasn't a house for a family. The cheery house on the beach was a place to heal for female teens suffering from psychiatric issues. I glanced over at my mom, who was waiting on me to make the first move. She'd packed my things with me in silence after I'd agreed with the psychiatrist that I was suffering from Post Traumatic Stress Disorder and needed help. I'd been ready to agree to anything to get me out of the office where it was obvious she really wanted me to change personalities on her or admit to cutting myself. I wasn't a psychopath and this seemed to be the one diagnosis she'd given me I was okay with lying about.

"Do you want to make a few phone calls before we go get you settled in? One of the rules is you can't have your phone here." Mom's expression told me she was afraid the news of no phone was going to be a deal breaker for me. I nodded thinking of Leif and Miranda. I needed to let them know where I would be for a while. Mom nodded. "Okay. I'll start taking your bags on up and getting you all checked in." She said the words with a small hiccup as if she were about to break down and cry. She'd handled this all so well and been so strong, thinking this was what I needed.

I reached over and took her hand and squeezed it tightly. "Mom, I'm okay with this. I think it's going to help me. Don't look so upset. It's all going to be okay." She nodded with tears filling her eyes. I knew I had to get better for her. I had to find a way to live with the hole in my chest.

Mom headed up the stairs with my bags in her hands and I picked up my phone and dialed Miranda first.

"Well, it's about flippen' time I see your name pop up on my screen. Jeez! Pagan, you've been scaring me."

I smiled at the relief in her voice. "I'm sorry." I took a deep breath. "I've been diagnosed with Post Traumatic Stress Disorder. I'm waiting to be checked into this rehabilitation center for people with similar issues. I can't keep my phone but I was told I could have visitors if you want to come see me sometime." Miranda was silent and I started to wonder if my phone had dropped her call.

"So, they can fix you...I mean, this?" she asked slowly sounding as if she was terrified.

"Yes, they can." I told her reassuringly. But I knew they couldn't heal me. I would never be fixed. I would just learn to go through the motions of living so those I loved didn't worry about me.

"Have you told Leif?" Her voice had lost its earlier cheer and I hated that it was my fault.

"No, I called you first."

With a ragged sigh she said, "I love you." I felt tears spring into my eyes for the first time. I loved her too. "Call Leif and I'll be there to visit ASAP."

"Okay. See you soon. Bye." I pressed end and then called Leif.

"Pagan." He sounded as relieved as Miranda had.

"Hey you," I said, needing to reassure him before I dealt him the same news I'd just given Miranda.

"You feeling better today? I hope so, Pagan, because I'm missing you like mad." I smiled at the warmth his voice always caused.

"I have Post Traumatic Stress Disorder, Leif. I went to see a psychiatrist."

"What is that? Are they giving you medicine to fix it?" His voice sounded panicked.

"It's exactly what it sounds like. I'm having trouble functioning normally due to the trauma we all experienced. You all handled it normally. I didn't. It could be a chemical imbalance; they're not sure. But I'm going to be in a psychiatric center for a while. They're supposed to be able to fix me here. I'm not going to be able to keep my phone but I can have visitors."

Leif seemed to be taking a deep breath. "So I can come see you? How long will you be there?"

"Yes, you can, and I'm not sure yet."

"I'm sorry this is happening to you, Pagan. I'm so sorry." His voice sounded full of pain and guilt.

"Listen to me, Leif. I'm dealing with this because of things that are wrong with me. What we saw just triggered it. I'll get better." I needed to hear that lie as much as he did. After reassuring him several more times I hung up and left my phone on the passenger seat of the car. My overnight bag was all that was left in the back seat so I grabbed it and headed up the stairs to my new home, at least for now.

The pale yellow room I'd been assigned contained one small round window overlooking the beach. I'd hugged my mother good-bye downstairs thirty minutes ago. I reminded myself I was doing this for her. It would help her deal with her fears of my being crazy. And being away from my bedroom, where so many memories of Dank existed, would help me find a way to live without him.

An older lady stood outside on the sand with a bag of what looked like sandwich bread, throwing it into the air while seagulls circled her head. Either she wasn't a local and didn't realize that was a really good way to get pooped on, or she was a psychiatric

Abbi Glines

patient who was too mental to care about a little bird poop.

I turned away from the growing flurry of hungry birds and studied the small room at least half the size of a regular bedroom. Considering this place held twenty-five patients at one time, and ten nurses and two doctors, the rooms couldn't be too big even if the house was a really large two-story. A single bed sat in the middle of the room with a small, round, white table holding a shell-covered lamp. One single oval mirror hung on the wall over a dresser with three drawers. A very small closet, only large enough to hang up fifteen items and hold three pairs of shoes, was on the opposite wall. I was only allowed one hour in my room during the day. I could use it all at one time or spread it out throughout the day. It was their way of keeping patients surrounded by other people. Seclusion bred depression was their rule of thumb around here.

I glanced over at the small alarm clock they'd left on the round table. I had used up ten of my minutes in my room. I needed to go walk around and be seen so I would have time left to come back later. I walked into the hallway and closed my door behind me. The small key they'd given me was in my pocket and I locked my door. Apparently, there was cause to worry about theft with some of the patients. You weren't allowed to bring anything of value with you but those suffering from personality disorders would take anything and I needed my clothing. I'd only been allotted a small amount and I needed what I had.

A door opened up down the hallway and a girl with bushy, brown hair and large round glasses stared at me, and then quickly slammed her door shut. I heard the lock click behind her. She was easily startled and frightened. She must be someone truly suffering from Post Traumatic Stress Disorder or PTSD as they referred to it here. I stared at the other closed doors wondering if everyone on this hall had the same disorder. If so it was going to be loud at night with the screaming caused by nightmares.

I walked down the stairs to the main living area, or what they referred to as the Great Room. It was where the televisions played sitcoms and board games were set up on tables. There were no computers or internet available for patients. A nurse smiled at me brightly as she walked by with a basket full of snack foods.

"We'll be eating our afternoon snack soon. Hang around in here and you can get something to eat and meet some of the other patients. We have several your age." Meeting teenagers with psychi-

atric disorders wasn't really appealing to me. But I didn't say anything. Instead, I walked to the double glass doors leading out onto
the front deck.

"You won't be able to open them. They lock them. You know,
for us crazies who may take a wild notion to see if we can fly. Although, I figure the sand isn't going to kill us when we hit." I turned
around to see a young girl with bleached blond hair that I guessed
was probably shoulder length. She had it pulled up in piggy tales
on top of her head. She wore bright red lipstick, which stood out
against her pale skin.

"Thanks."

She shrugged. "No problem. If you want to go outside and enjoy
the beach you can get a nurse to go with you. They like having an
excuse to go outside." I remembered the lady outside earlier feed-
ing the birds. She'd been alone.

I didn't really want to know who she was so I again nodded and
said, "Thanks." She tilted her thin face from side to side and acted
as if she was examining something rather dramatically.

"You aren't a mental, are you?" I hadn't expected this strange
girl to make such an accurate observation. After all, the doctors all
believed I needed help. I shrugged, unsure how to respond.

"Well, they seem to think I am."

She raised the dark eyebrows she'd left out of the bleaching.
"They can be wrong. They have been before." I wondered if she was
referring to herself. I glanced over at the nurse who sat behind a
desk working on a laptop. She didn't seem to react to the accusation
that they had people in here who didn't belong. "Karen knows it's
true. She just won't admit it. Will you Nurse Karen?" The blond was
grinning at the nurse, who glanced up and rolled her eyes affectionately and went back to typing. "She knows it but she's too busy on
Twitter to admit it."

The nurse reached over and patted the stack of papers she had
beside her before glancing back up at the blond again. "I'm plug-
ging in meds and test results."

"Blah, blah, blah. Don't let her fool you, she's a Twitter whore.
On it all the fucking time."

The nurse shot her warning glance. "Language please. You'll
lose ten more minutes from your room time if you aren't careful."

The blond shrugged and stared back at me. "Like I said, they aren't always right around here. I can see it in your eyes. You're very sane. You don't have the demons in your eyes most of the people here do." She stood up and stretched, showing a very pale, flat stomach. She had a large black bar through her belly button. "I'm Gee, by the way." She held out her hand for me to shake and I went to return it and she jerked her hand away. "Rule number one, don't shake anyone's hands. This place is full of mentals."

I smiled. "I take it you aren't one of them."

She let out a cackle of laughter. "Oh no, I'm as screwed up as they come." She sauntered away and slapped the papers the nurse was working on as she walked by. "Don't Tweet too much, Karen, it's bad for the eyes. Gotta pull back off that shit."

"Ten minutes, Gee," the nurse said without looking up.

Gee glanced back at me and winked. "They don't like dirty words so if you have a shitty mouth you need to reign it in."

"Twenty minutes, Gee," the nurse said again, still focused on the screen. Gee cackled with laughter again and headed back toward the dining room.

The nurse glanced up at me. "Gee is definitely a special case. You'll learn to ignore her. It's snack time in the dining hall if you want to go get something to eat and meet some other patients."

I smiled. "Thank you, but I'm not real hungry. Can I just stay here and watch the television?" Nurse Karen nodded and went back to her work. I curled up in a chair and stared blankly at the television screen feeling lonelier than ever before.

# Chapter Sixteen

The dining hall was a large room with five long tables that sat ten people each. A cafeteria-style buffet was set up where nurses filled the patients' plates. This was the only room with large windows. The entire south wall was primarily several large picture windows overlooking the beach. I thanked the nurse as she handed me the bright red tray filled with macaroni and cheese, which appeared very edible, grilled chicken strips, a Caesar salad, green beans, a large wheat roll, and a small slice of some sort of custard I already knew I wouldn't be trying. The tables closest to the windows seemed to be the popular ones as they were already filling up and a few patients were bickering over specific locations. I decided to sit at one of the tables away from the windows. I didn't want to have to deal with sitting in someone's coveted seat. I took a plastic cup full of iced tea and turned toward the back row of tables.

"You prolly wanna go get yerself some of that sugah. That tea ain't got no sweet in it and it is just nasty without it." A girl with stringy, brown hair and big, brown, round eyes stood frowning at the cup in my hand. Her front teeth seemed to stick out a little and her nose was covered in freckles. She reminded me of someone you might find on a farm somewhere.

"Oh, um, thanks but I don't drink sugar in my iced tea," I explained and she snarled her nose.

"Ya must be a Floridian then. Ain't figerd out why you people carry on as if ya from up north. Ya'll are more suthurn than we are in Mississippi and we know iced tea needs sugah."

I struggled to understand her accent but I smiled and turned back toward the table I'd been heading for when I noticed it now had two other occupants: the girl with the brown, bushy hair who had slammed the door and locked herself inside after seeing me earlier, and Gee. I faltered and wondered if maybe I should go sit at another table when Gee shot me a challenging grin. I figured I'd better stick to my plan. Gee expected me to go somewhere else and I didn't want her thinking she scared me. I was a little surprised she was sitting with the jumpy girl. Gee didn't seem like the kind of person a fearful, nervous person would be drawn to.

"Ya aint thinkin uh sittin over with those two, are ya?" the farm girl asked me.

I shrugged. "I don't see why not."

She chuckled. "Cause Gee is a nut case, that's why. Straight looney toons, I tell ya." I bit back a smile at the fact this place was for the mentally disturbed. Wasn't everyone a little looney toons?

"Um, thanks, but I've met Gee and she seems fine." The girl beside me stared at me as if studying me carefully.

"You ain't a Schizo, too, are ya? 'Cause I need to know. I ain't comfortable round no Schizo's." I glanced back at Gee and wondered if that was what she was. Did she have Schizophrenia?

I shook my head. "No, I'm PTSD."

She beamed. "Oh, good I can deal with that. Ya'll are easy to handle. Me, I'm Bipolar. Mama had me brought in cause I tried to knock myself off a while back."

I stiffened, looking at this friendly person with the innocent farm girl appearance, wondering how someone like her could attempt to end her life. "Why?" I heard myself ask.

She shrugged. "Sometimes I get so sad that it jest sounds good." She said this with all seriousness and I shivered. I never realized there were kids my age who appeared normal but dealt with so much internally. I sat my tray down across from the bushy brunette. "Nice to talk to ya," the farm girl said, smiling.

"Not going to sit near me, Henrietta? Why, Henrietta, I do believe my feelings are hurt. I may feel the need to cry right here in front of the whole damn cafeteria," Gee said, smiling at the retreating form of the farm girl.

"Leave her alone," the bushy brunette hissed before sticking a spoon full of macaroni and cheese into her mouth.

Gee grinned back at the bushy brunette. "It's so much fun to tease Henrietta. Sometimes I can even get her to say 'I've had 'nough uh yer smack talkin'. Now leave me uhlone Gee fer I tell on ya'." Gee imitated Henrietta's speech perfectly. The bushy brunette grinned and swallowed her mouthful of food.

"So you aren't crazy? I'm Jess, sorry about earlier today but I'm not into meeting the new crazies who come. I'm crazy enough and I don't need any more crazy around me. I spend too much time with Gee as it is." Gee grinned and stuck out her tongue, which also had a bar in it but this one was silver. I stared, surprised by the appearance of her tongue and she cackled with laughter.

"Relax. Pagan. I don't bite, at least, I don't bite other people." She laughed at her comment as did her partner. "I told Jess not to get all worked up over you. I'd seen you and there wasn't anything wrong with you. But you're interesting. We can't seem to figure out what it is they seem to think you have."

I moved the food around on my plate but nothing appealed to me.

"PTSD," I supplied, glancing up at her.

"Ah, so they think you have had trauma and it screwed with you. What's really wrong, since we know you're not a crazy? What did you do to get sent here?" Jess asked before jamming another spoon full of macaroni and cheese into her mouth. I glanced back toward the nurses who had now started patrolling the aisles.

"That isn't something I really want to discuss." I picked up my roll, hoping if I started filling my mouth they would stop expecting me to talk.

Gee nodded and then nudged Jess in the side. "Look over at Roberta. She's about to take out Kim for touching her plate. Ah, damn, there is Nurse Karen. She's taking Roberta to get a new plate and wash her hands." Gee grinned over at me. "Roberta is the best kind of mental case to mess with."

"She is OCD," Jess finished for her, grinning. Apparently poor Roberta's problem was a point of entertainment. Gee flicked her tongue ring on her teeth.

"Funny shit," she said, grinning.

"Ten minutes tomorrow, Gee," Nurse Karen's voice came from behind me.

Jess rolled her eyes. "Why do you do that when you know she can hear you?"

Gee shrugged. "'Cause I can. Or 'cause I don't like going to my room alone. You know the voices in my head get a little too loud when I'm alone." Gee flashed a grin at me and took a bite of her custard pie.


I was relieved to get into the bed. After dinner we had been sent to meeting rooms for 'Discussion Time', which meant they encouraged everyone to talk. I didn't want to talk. I had nothing to say. It had grown so tiresome that I'd found myself watching out for wandering souls. After no sign of one for hours, I realized I hadn't seen one since I stepped foot into the house. Apparently souls were scared of this place. I couldn't blame them. I could hear the waves crashing outside and I hoped that was the only sound I heard tonight.

As if on cue, I heard a muffled scream. I cringed and buried myself under the covers. It wasn't that they scared me, but I hurt for them. They truly dealt with things I didn't understand. Another scream echoed down the hall. Someone had opened their door and set their terror loose. I glanced back at my door to make sure I'd locked it. A nurse was talking to the screamer and several doors opened and closed.

"I'm never going to be able to sleep," I mumbled into the darkness. I got out of bed and walked over to the window to watch the moonlit waves crashing against the shoreline. The waves reminded me of the last night I'd spent with Dank. He'd saved me from the waves intent on taking my life. I'd been ready for it to happen until his arm had wrapped around me. Pain pierced my heart and I had to sit back down on the bed and hold my stomach tightly in order to hold myself together. Another scream came from a few rooms away. A hot tear trickled down my face. I was alone for the first time in my life. I laid down with my knees pulled up to my chest and my arms wrapped tightly around them. My eyelids grew heavy and the muffled screams began to be drowned away.

As I drifted into my dreams the music began to play. I fought to wake back up. The familiar music was my lullaby. The weariness from the day and my sense of loneliness seemed to disappear as the music played. The warmth of Dank's voice filled my mind and I slept.

"Already got a visitor and he's yummy, yummy, lick your lips yummy," Gee said, strutting into the library I was almost positive she never spent any time in. I glanced up from the worn leather copy of Pride and Prejudice I'd found among the shelves of books lining the walls.

"I have a visitor?" It had to be Leif. "Thank you." I stood up and followed Gee back down to the Great Room where all visitations had to take place. Leif's frown evaporated when he saw me coming toward him. A smile eased the worried line in his forehead.

"Pagan," he said walking up and pulling me into a fierce hug. I held onto him tightly, trying hard not to cry.

"I'm so glad you came," I whispered, hoping the emotion in my voice wasn't obvious.

"I miss you, Pagan, so bad," he said into my hair and we stood there holding onto each other until someone cleared their throat and I reluctantly pulled back. Nurse Karen was frowning and she shook her head.

"Oh, come on Twitter whore this is more entertaining than the shit we have to watch on television." Gee called from her chair.

"Twenty minutes, Gee," Nurse Karen replied with boredom.

"I already lost all my fucking time today, Nurse Karen."

She glared and pointed a finger toward Gee. "Twenty minutes tomorrow and you will lose all privileges for a week if you say one more bad word."

Gee rolled her eyes and patted the seat beside her. "Come bring Mr. Yummy over here so I can look at him," she said with a purr to her voice.

"Gee, go help Nurse Ashley with the lunch preparations."

Gee glared at Karen and stood up with a sulk. "I was gonna play nice, you know, Karen. You're just no fun, no fun at all." Gee licked her lips as she passed by Leif and winked at me. I squeezed Leif's hand and led him over to the farthest end of the Great Room where no television or board games were set up. It was always empty.

Leif studied me with concern. "Are all the people here like her?" He appeared traumatized. I chuckled and started to shake my head and thought better of it.

"No, but then she isn't the worst one here." Leif still appeared horrified. I smiled.

"They're very entertaining once you realize they're harmless. I feel so bad for them, Leif." I shook my head. "Anyway, tell me about school and Miranda and you. How is everyone?"

Leif's face eased into a relieved smile. "You seem better already." He touched the side of my head gently. "God, I've missed you."

"I miss you too. Thanks for coming today. I needed to talk to someone from the outside world. Tell me, how is everyone?"

He gave me a sad smile. "We're worried about you. We miss you and we talk about you all the time. Absolutely nothing else is going on." I wanted to tell him I thought about them all the time, too, but the truth was I thought about Dank. I'd heard him last night. He'd been there, in my dreams.

"Did you bring my schoolwork?" I asked, glancing at the bag in his hands.

"Oh, yes, here you go. Can you actually do it here?" He glanced over at the two girls who'd recently walked in and started playing Monopoly. Apparently, they were having a disagreement and had proceeded to shove play money down each other's shirts while yelling. Nurse Karen rushed over and started breaking the argument up. I heard her tell them how much alone time they'd lost.

"Why does she keep threatening everyone with time? Is that like how long you get time out or something?"

I laughed and shook my head. "No, it's actually the opposite. We only get one hour a day to stay in our rooms alone. It's a punishment to get your time deducted. Time alone in your room to escape is coveted."

Leif let out a ragged sigh and shook his head. "You don't belong here, Pagan," he said, staring back at me with a frown.

I shrugged. "Just because I don't throw fits, curse at nurses, and deal with voices in my head doesn't mean I'm not dealing with my own stuff." He didn't nod in agreement. His hand squeezed mine.

"I love you. I'm not going anywhere," he said in a hoarse whisper. Tears sprang to my eyes and I gave him a watery smile.

"I know." I wanted to say more but I knew I couldn't.

"Romeo, Romeo, wherefore art thou, Romeo," Gee called from the hallway as she walked toward the stairs with her arms full of towels.

I laughed out loud. "She's harmless," I assured Leif, and then thought about it a moment. "Okay, maybe not harmless. But she doesn't mean any harm right now." Leif's look of horror returned.

"Do you lock your door at night?" he asked, glancing around as if afraid one of them would hear him and come after him.

I grinned and nodded. "But only because there's a lot of screaming and running at night. Night terrors and the like."

He shook his head and gazed back down at me. "Please, hurry and get better and come home. This is not where you belong."

"I know."


The muffled screams began right after lights out was announced. I covered my head and blocked out the sound. I had waited all day to return to this bed and fall into a deep sleep where I could hopefully hear his music. I thought of the times he had sung to me and the times he'd held me and kissed me. My eyes drifted closed and the music began. I fought, wanting to open my eyes and find him in my room. He was there. I could feel him. His guitar played my lullaby and I tried desperately to open my eyes. It was as if a dark blanket was over me, and I couldn't remove. Instead of being panicked, it warmed me. The comfort of knowing Dank was with me would be enough for now. His voice joined the strumming of his guitar. He knew I was here and he'd come to me. I wasn't alone. The muffled sounds of screams and slamming doors ceased and all I heard was the music that helped fill the hole inside of me. I wanted to turn around and face the source of the music and throw myself into his arms. I drifted off to sleep, unable to fight the drowsiness any longer.

"Aren't you just little Miss Popularity?" Gee was sauntering down the hall toward my room when I stepped out into the hall after a thirty minute nap. If it wasn't for my nights when the music came and Dank was with me, I would lose my mind from the monotony of this place. "I have a visitor?" I asked as Gee turned into her bedroom.

"Yep," she said and slammed the door behind her. There was no way Gee had any alone time left today. I'd personally heard Nurse Karen take away two days' worth since breakfast. Someone would be up searching for her in a few minutes.

I headed down the steps, anxious to see who'd come to see me. The moment my eyes found Miranda standing at the front door with her arms crossed over her chest defensively I broke into a run.

"Did Gee come tell you that you had a visitor?" Nurse Karen asked, frowning and glancing behind me. I nodded, not wanting to be the one to rat Gee out for going to her room. "Where is she?" Nurse Karen asked.

I raised my eyebrows and shrugged. "I thought she came back down here." Nurse Karen stared down the hallway, frowning as if she thought she had missed Gee's return. She nodded and went back to typing on the computer.

Miranda threw her arms around me as soon as I reached her. It felt so good to see her. "Please leave with me," she whispered in my ear.

I chuckled. "I can't."

"I'll help you break out. Girl, these people are crazy, you need to get out." I bit back a laugh. "The Gee girl is a nut case and she did not come back down those stairs. I was watching her. If she didn't come back down with you promptly I was coming up to avenge you." I laughed out loud this time.

"Come on over here and we can talk." I took her hand and led her back to where I had sat with Leif two days ago.

Miranda glanced back at the stairs. "She still hasn't come back down. Maybe you need to tell the nurse," Miranda hissed from behind me. I sat down in a chair and pointed at the one beside me.

"No, I'm not telling Karen anything. Gee isn't bad. She really likes to leave an impression. It's more about attention with her. And I don't want to be the one to rat her out. She likes me and I'd like to keep it that way. I've seen what she does to the people she doesn't like." Miranda's brown eyes grew big and round. I smiled reassuringly. "Things a school bully would do, not an axe murderer, calm down."

Miranda seemed to relax a little and crossed her legs in front of her then leaned forward to stare at me closely. "So, they are being okay to you here? The crazies like you and no one is mistreating you? Because if they are I'm going to take them down. There isn't a mental around here gonna mess with my girl. I got your back." Her fierce expression warmed me.

I smiled. "Everyone is great, but thanks for the support."

She peered over her shoulder at Nurse Karen, "I hope the other nurses pay more attention to the mental cases than that one does. Do you know she's playing around on Twitter?"

# Chapter Seventeen

"Pagan." Doctor Janice walked into the Great Room where I sat playing Monopoly with Gee, who cheats, and Roberta, who keeps glaring at Gee for cheating.

"Yes, Ma'am?" I asked. She smiled at the girls with me and held up a clipboard in her hands.

"It's time for your assessment. Please come with me." I stood up from my Indian- style position on the floor.

"Ah, shit, I was so enjoying you, Peggy Ann, and here you're gonna be told you're not mental and sent home." Gee flicked her pierced tongue at me and winked. She'd taken to calling me Peggy Ann the last few days. It was slightly annoying but it wasn't worth making it an issue. I forced a smile and followed the doctor. I wasn't ready to leave yet. Dank came to me at night and I feared once I was home he would leave me again. My chest ached, reminding me it was still empty. Doctor Janice opened the door to her office and held it for me to enter.

"You will have to ignore the mess on my desk. I've been going through charts this week and it always gets a little out of hand in here." She smiled at me apologetically and walked around to stand behind her desk. "Please have a seat," she said, motioning to the overstuffed black leather chairs beside me. I sank down onto one as Doctor Janice took the clipboard in her hands. She slipped the pair of glasses hanging from her neck on a pearl chain onto the bridge of her large nose.

"It appears, Pagan, that you're the most mentally healthy patient we've had in a very long time. You're compassionate and make friends with even some of our harder cases, which only strengthens the diagnosis that you are not mentally ill. Befriending someone like Georgia Vain isn't easy, and Jess is her only friend because she happens to suffer from fear of Georgia and self-preservation. The evaluations from the nurses all say you're kind and understanding. You react the way one does who understands you're surrounded by those with mental sicknesses and you're patient with them. That not only makes you a very pleasant patient but also a very stable person." Doctor Janice sat the clipboard down on her desk and slipped the glasses off and carefully dropped them back on her chest. "The basic fact is: you don't belong here."

Abbi Glines

I nodded, knowing there was no point in arguing with the doctor that I was a mental case and needed to stay. Doctor Janice glanced back down at the chart in front of her. "I carefully looked over the recommendation sent when you were prescribed a stay here to help you learn to deal with the trauma you suffered. I don't normally disagree so strongly with other doctors' observations but this time you were grossly misdiagnosed. Now, the question that fascinates me is why, Pagan Moore, did you get so withdrawn in yourself that your mother sought medical attention for you?"

I swallowed the fear building inside of me at the thought that I would be sent home today and tonight I wouldn't have Dank. I needed a reason to stay. I stared back at Doctor Janice and wondered if I could be honest with her and if the truth would keep me here. If I told her I saw dead people, would she change her mind? I started to speak and an image of my mom's tear-filled eyes when she'd come to visit yesterday came back to me. She missed me and was worried about me. I was hurting her, or rather the sickness she thought I had was hurting her. If I admitted to seeing souls they would indeed label me crazy. I would be diagnosed with a whole new problem and my mother would be consumed with worry. I would just try to get one more night. One more chance to hear Dank and this time I'd fight the heavy sleep that always kept me from seeing him. I would find a way to speak to him.

"The car accident bothered me and I did withdraw into myself because I didn't like thinking about what I'd witnessed. I agreed to come here to make my mom feel better. I was scaring her with the way I'd become reclusive. My stay here has been eye opening and I will always cherish it. The girls here are just like me but they have mental sicknesses that make living a normal life difficult. They're still people. They still have feelings and want to be accepted. I've enjoyed getting to know all of them. You're right, I don't have the mental sicknesses the other patients do, but being around them has helped me learn to accept what I witnessed."

Doctor Janice smiled. "Well, that continues to confirm my diagnosis. You're completely mentally sane and very mature for your age. Would you like to call your mother and tell her you're free to go home?" This was my moment to ask for one more night. I needed to say goodbye. I needed to open my eyes tonight and see him. I couldn't leave until I'd seen him.

"Doctor Janice, would it be a problem if I stayed tonight and left

Existence

first thing in the morning? I would like to have dinner with my new friends and properly say farewell to everyone."

Doctor Janice gave me a slow, pleased smiled and nodded. "I think that would be perfect."

I glanced at the phone on her desk. "Can I go ahead and call my mom, then, and let her know I'll be free to go in the morning?" I thought of how the news I could come home in the morning was going to bring back a smile to her face. Knowing she would be relieved eased the ache some, but not enough.

I carried my tray of food over to sit across from Gee and Jess. Gee tilted her head from side to side like she so often did when she was thinking about something, and flicked her tongue ring against her teeth several times.

"You're leaving, aren't you, Peggy Ann?" I smiled at her and nodded. She sighed dramatically. "Figures they'd send you home since you have no mental cracks. I mean, you don't even scream at night. Then, of course, he sings to you. Kind of impresses me really. He'd scare the shit out of me if he came in my room. You may not be a screw ball but the fact you're not scared of him makes you someone I don't want to piss off."

I froze, listening to her words. She knew Dank came to me at night and sang to me. How did she know? Did she see him? Did she see souls? Was that my problem? Was I Schizo? She cackled her mad laughter and winked at me.

"You're thinking you might just be whack after all, aren't you, Peggy Ann? You wish you were this fucked up. No dice though, girlie. No fuckin' dice," she whispered leaning toward me so the nurses wouldn't hear her cursing and take away anymore of her privileges.

"What're you carrying on about? Did you take your meds today, Gee, 'cause you're talking off your head worse than normal," Jess said, frowning before shoveling black eyed peas into her mouth. Gee didn't take her eyes off me. She almost had a glimmer in her eyes as she watched me, enjoying the confusion I knew was clear on my face.

"Only the ones he has come for can see him, Peggy Ann. You know that right? Only the ones whose time is near. I know why he's here." She tilted her head side to side and stared at me closely. "But he doesn't sing to me. No, he doesn't sing to me."

Jess sighed loudly and glared at Gee. "If you don't shut up talking like a psychopath I'm calling Nurse Karen over here to drug your ass," she grumbled.

"Who is he?" I asked Gee quietly, afraid she truly didn't know.

A sad smile touched her red lips and she shook her head. "Ah, so he isn't coming for you then. So very odd. You see him and he is with you so much yet he hasn't come for you. He is the only one who can tell you." Gee stood up, leaving her tray untouched on the table, and walked away.

Jess stared at me and shook her head sadly. "She's hiding her meds under her tongue again and spitting them out in the toilet. I'm going to have to tell someone before she gets any crazier. I'm guessing if she goes too long without her meds she could do something fatal." Jess took a bite of meatloaf, stood up, and went over to Nurse Ashley.

Tonight I was resolved to ask him again but the fear that it would drive him away scared me more than the words from my psychotic friend.


I packed the last pair of jeans into my suitcase and zipped it up. The drawers were empty and the closet no longer held any of my things. I walked over to the small, round table and took the cards Leif and Miranda had sent me. Reading them each morning had given me a reason to smile. I slipped them into the pocket of my overnight bag and sat down on my bed. I had been given permission to come to my room as early as I wanted. The rules of seclusion no longer applied to me and I'd needed to pack. The small room wasn't much bigger than my mom's walk-in closet but it was going to be hard to walk away from in the morning. Just like at home, this bedroom had held Dank. It would hold the memories of him.

Nurse Ashley was walking the halls, ringing her bell for the lights out announcement. I stood up and pulled back the covers on my bed and slipped inside before reaching over and turning out the lamp. Tonight he would come and I would talk to him. I wouldn't have to worry he would leave me and not return because I was leaving in the morning. I wanted to know why Gee knew who he was or if she thought he was someone else. Was he the same 'he' the little red-headed girl at the hospital had spoken of? The 'he' she had said was coming to take her soon.

Dank had been the one to take the couple from the car fire at their death. Is that what he did? Was he the soul who went and retrieved other souls when they died? I closed my eyes and waited. I thought of the different things I'd seen and what Gee and the little girl had said. It all pointed to Dank being a guardian of some kind. Maybe an angel. I turned back and forth, waiting for the music. Waiting for Dank to come and sing to me.

He never came.

The morning sun cast a glow across the pale yellow room as I stood with my bags, glancing around to see if I'd missed anything. I was leaving without answers. My thoughts went back to Gee. I slipped my overnight bag up higher on my shoulder and headed downstairs to find her. I wanted to talk to her one last time before I left. To tell her goodbye and to ask her once more if she could explain to me who it was she thought she heard in my room. The Great Room was empty and the sounds of chatter drifted from the dining hall, where everyone was eating breakfast. Gee would be there. I sat my bags down beside the door and went to say my final goodbyes.

The moment I walked into the busy dining room I glanced over to the far table. Jess sat alone at the end, staring down at her plate as she shoveled food into her mouth. I glanced back at the serving line and the nurses had finished serving the patients. Everyone was sitting down at their tables to eat. Nurse Karen peered up and nodded toward me with a sad smile on her face. I walked over to Jess and sat down across from her.

"She's gone," Jess said as she shoveled another bite of cheese grits into her mouth.

"Gee's gone? What do you mean?" I asked, confused. I had just seen her before I'd gone up to bed last night, sitting with a group of other girls playing a card game.

Jess lifted her gaze up at me and frowned. "She went whack on them this morning about four. Started screaming and cursing and they had to sedate her. She's getting worse and Doctor Janice won't keep the ones that get so disturbed they become dangerous to themselves. She transfers them to the hospital where they can be kept on the looney floor under lock and key." Jess shook her head and took a big gulp of chocolate milk. "I knew she'd be shipped off soon enough. The Schizos always are."

I felt a sick knot in my stomach. "Do you know what hospital she was sent to?"

Jess shrugged. "No, 'cause I ain't crazy enough to get shipped there."

I stood up. "Well, okay. Um, it was really nice to get to know you, Jess." Telling her I would see her later sounded strange because we both knew it wasn't true. So I simply smiled and said, "Goodbye." She nodded, stuffed her mouth with a piece of bacon, and gazed past me toward the windows overlooking the Gulf. I turned and headed toward the door. Nurse Karen walked toward me.

"I'll need your mom to sign some release papers," she said, following me toward the door.

I turned to her. "Gee was sent to the hospital?" I wanted to hear it from a nurse.

"I'm afraid so. She isn't safe here. She needs a tighter leash than what we can offer in this setting." I swallowed the sudden lump in my throat and walked beside her down the hall. My mom was waiting to greet me. She stood in the Great Room watching us as we approached. I peered over my shoulder at Nurse Karen before we were close enough for my mother to hear.

"What hospital is she at?" I wanted to see her.

Nurse Karen smiled at me. "Mercy Medical." The hospital where I had signed on to volunteer. However, now that I had a record of mental issues they wouldn't let me work at the hospital anymore. I was pretty sure I could still visit.

"Pagan, you look as if you have lost ten pounds," Mom said as soon as I was close enough to hear her. She walked toward me and wrapped her arms around me, holding on tightly. "I'm so happy you're coming home. We'll put some weight back on you in no time."

I smiled and enjoyed the comfort of her arms. "I'm sure the pizza and Chinese will be limitless," I teased, and she laughed, pulling back from me.

"Never said I would cook the food that puts the weight back on you." Her eyes were watery but I knew it wasn't sad tears this time.

# Chapter Eighteen

I stood staring at the kitchen table covered with empty soda cans, two empty pizza boxes, and half of a chocolate cake which had read: "Welcome Home, Pagan," in white icing on top. Leif, Miranda, and Wyatt had surprised me this evening. I'd opened the door four hours ago to find the three of them holding pizza, sodas, and a bakery box. Being with the three of them, eating food with real taste, and entertaining them with stories from my time at the mental house had made it really feel like I was home. Their smiling faces and familiar laughter had warmed me from the coldness always penetrating me. Leif had held me as we sat in the living room, catching up on everything I'd missed. Kendra had fallen off the pyramid during cheerleading practice and had a cast on her right leg. Miranda appeared much too pleased about the girl's predicament. College scouts had come to the playoff game to watch Leif and he now had scholarship offers from two different colleges.

Life had gone on without me. Knowing Leif would be okay when I was no longer a part of his life eased some of the guilt inside me. I couldn't keep him. Not when I ached for Dank so badly. Even if I couldn't find Dank, I knew he cared. He would come back eventually. He had known I needed him and he'd come to me. Even if I couldn't see him, I knew he was near. I glanced up the stairs knowing he wouldn't come tonight. My room was a safe place for me now. If I could just see him and tell him I love him and I will go wherever I have to in order to be with him... But he wouldn't allow me to even know or understand.

I threw the empty soda cans into the recycling bin at the back door and headed upstairs to go to bed. Today had been exhausting and I would be returning to school tomorrow. The empty desk where Dank had once sat in English Literature flashed in my mind and the hole in my chest ached.


The music was playing. It took me a moment as I opened my eyes to realize Dank was playing my lullaby. I sat straight up in bed and looked to the chair to find it empty, yet the music was playing. It took me a moment to realize through my sleepy haze that the music wasn't in my room or even in the house. The music drifted through the open window from outside. I jumped and ran to see where it was coming from. Was Dank out there? The back yard was dark and foggy. The music drifted up to me from somewhere in the night. I reached for my jacket, slipped on my shoes, and then headed downstairs and out the back door, closing it gently behind me so as not to wake my mom. If she caught me wandering around in the dark she may pack me back up and return me to the mental house.

The music sounded as if it was coming from the woods. I went over to the garden shed to find a flashlight. I knew mom kept one on the shelf over the potting table. Once I found it and checked to see if the batteries were good, I headed back into the dark yard.

Why would Dank be out here in the dark playing my lullaby? I stepped onto the path my mom had made so she could take nature walks from our back yard to the community pond through the woods. The leaves crackled around me and I bit back a squeal. I needed to find Dank before some strange critter found me. The music drew me deeper into the woods. My flashlight only helped marginally. The thick fog made visibility almost zero. I kept chanting in my head that Dank was out here somewhere. He wanted me to find him. Why else would he play his music so I could hear it, if not to draw me out here?

A light glimmered in the darkness, peeking through the fog. I walked toward it, knowing the music was coming from that spot. The closer I got, the brighter the light grew. I broke through the fog and into a small clearing. A glowing ball floated inside the circle of trees surrounding the clearing. I tucked the flashlight into the pocket of my jacket before taking a cautious step toward the orb of light. Dank's music was coming from the light.

Confused, I quickly scanned the clearing for Dank. It remained empty, but for me and the musical light. Why was it playing Dank's music? Fear slowly began to trickle through me. Dank wasn't here. He would never draw me out into the dark woods alone. Someone else would. Someone who wanted me to leave my bed and wander out away from the protection of my home.

"Thump thump, thump thump, that heart of yours sure is racing, isn't it, Peggy Ann?" I spun around at the sound of Gee's voice. She stood in the far corner of the clearing, watching me. She didn't look like the Gee in the mental house. Her short blond hair was flying around in the night breeze loosely and her red lips now seemed to shimmer like silver glitter in the moonlight. I took a step back, wanting to put distance between us.

"What are you doing, Gee?" I asked, attempting to keep the panic out of my voice. She puckered her shimmering lips and tilted her head from side to side.

"Hmmm. Little Miss. Smarty Pants isn't so smart after all. The only sane girl in the house, HA! You were the only one stupid enough to be my friend." I searched frantically around me trying to think of a way to escape.

"Jess was your friend," I replied, wanting to stall her while I tried to think of how I could get away from her.

Gee began to cackle. "Jess is a lunatic whose mind I easily controlled. You, however, came near me without any help from me. You did it all on your own. You trusted me." She stopped talking and began drawing closer to me, laughing maniacally. "I'd been sent to right the wrong. I was there because of you. The first night I was going to take you. It was meant to be," she snarled. "But he was there already. I hadn't even killed you yet and he was there. Protecting you. Foolish human that you are. The simple soul living inside of you. He protects it."

She began pacing back and forth in front of me as if she were a large cat stalking her prey. I took another step back and she laughed wickedly as if my attempting to leave was as insane as she was. "It's his *JOB*! I was sent to fix his wrong! He broke a rule with you. He can't break the rules. If he doesn't right this wrong then he'll pay. It must be corrected." She began tilting her head back and forth again, studying me as if I were an unknown specimen. I realized her eyes no longer looked insane but more like those of a cat. Her features had all taken on a glow. She wasn't human. She wasn't a mental patient. She was...something else.

"What are you Gee?" I asked.

She smiled. "You really want to know?" She stopped stalking me and glanced around the clearing as if expecting someone else. Were there more like her out here? "I guess since it's your time you can know. You really should have known all along. Your time has long since passed. You're like an overdue library book. Tick tock, tick tock, you're costing me valuable time. This isn't my job. It is HIS," she hissed, scanning the clearing again and I realized she was waiting for Dank.

"Who's Dank?" I asked. She grinned at this question and raised one of her eyebrows that were now just as blond as her hair.

"Who do you think he is, Peggy Ann?" she taunted.

"He takes those who die on to wherever they are supposed to go," I replied in a whisper almost afraid to hear myself say the words. Gee began to cackle her maniacal laughter.

"Well, if you were correct then this would be all the much easier. But seeing as how you are slightly off, it makes this harder. Dank isn't a transporter. I am." I stood staring into her large, dark eyes that seemed to shimmer like her lips.

"That's right, Peggy Ann, I take them up or I take them down," she said with a snarl of distaste. "And you were going to be easy. You were going up. You would be given a new body and a new life and your soul would have done what good souls do. They live forever, over and over again. But NO!" She shouted into the darkness as red sparks flew from her fingertips. "NO, PAY-GAYN, that isn't want happened. WHY THE HELL NOT? Well this time your pretty little soul was in a pretty little young body and you had a lovely smile and a lovely walk and a lovely laugh and you were interesting. You could see other souls and you were *braaave* and blah, blah, blah. Whatever." She paused and glared at me. "You got to him. No one is supposed to get to him."

She began stalking back and forth in front of me again, watching me as if she wasn't sure what to do with me. "So, now it is me who has to right this wrong. He is too weak to do it. He wants you. He doesn't want to send your soul with me to go up and live a new life. He can't stand the thought of ending things for you." She rolled her eyes and threw her hands up in the air with a frustrated sigh. "I've been sent to get you, with or without his assistance. He'll be here in the end—don't frown. You'll see his sexy face again." Gee started walking toward me with her catlike prance.

"You didn't tell me who he is," I said, backing away from her.

"What is he? You still don't know? And here I thought I'd made it all very clear," she taunted, stopping right in front of me to run a red fingernail down my face. I shivered at the familiar, icy touch. The blond who had tried to drown me had felt like her.

"You tried to drown me," I said hoarsely, searching for some resemblance to the blond I'd thought Dank killed.

She grinned and shook her head, "No, Peggy Ann, that wasn't me. Ky was another transporter who your lover boy annihilated. You can see now why I'm not real fond of the job that has been entrusted to me. He isn't going to be happy with me. I don't want his anger directed my way when I snuff out his precious one. After all, who wants to fuck with Death." I swallowed against a sudden knot of fear in my throat.

"Death," I managed to whisper.

"Let her go." Dank's voice filled the clearing and Gee stiffened. Her grip went lax before it tightened again, this time with more intent. Breathing was now impossible.

"NO!" Dank's voice broke into the darkness. Gee's grip released as her body slammed flat against the ground. I gasped for air, staring down at her as she glared up at Dank with a mixture of fear and hate.

"It is time. I have been sent. You cannot break the rules. She is a soul that will be given another life. You can find her again. End this," Gee begged, glaring up at Dank. He stepped over her and reached a hand out to touch my neck. The warmth soothed the burning pain Gee's icy grip had left.

"I'm sorry," he whispered as he gazed down into my eyes. I nodded not sure what he was apologizing for, but I knew I would forgive him for anything. The wild cackle from behind him caused his dark blue eyes to transform into glowing sapphires. He turned and glared back at Gee. "Leave and I'll let you exist." His hard, cold demand penetrated the darkness.

Gee stood, watching him fearfully. "I can't leave until you do your job and I leave with that soul." Dank shook his head and his eyes seemed to cause her pain. She grimaced and stepped back. "Listen, I didn't ask to be the one who had to piss off Death. They sent me. I had no choice." She pointed at me. "I like her. I get what you see in her but she has to die. It is appointed."

Dank turned completely around and stalked toward her. "NOOOOO," he roared. Gee backed away with a terrified expression. I reached for Dank, grabbing his arm.

"No, Dank, please," I begged. He stopped and turned back at me.

"Do you understand what she wants? She isn't your friend, Pagan, although she played a very good role."

I stepped closer to him. "You're Death and I am supposed to die." I tore my eyes from his and looked at Gee. "And she is going to transport me."

Dank shook his head and glared back at Gee's relieved smile. "You made it sound that simple? You made her think she could just die and float away and have another life?" A growl rippled from his chest and Gee stepped farther away, her body visibly trembling. "It doesn't work that way, now does it, Gee?" he snarled, and I felt the muscles in his arms bulge under my touch.

"I'm here to right a wrong. You broke a rule that can't be broken. You can't keep her, Death. She's not a pet to play with. She's a soul and your only claim to a soul is the fact you take the body it lives in when the time is appointed. You do not own the souls."

"I will NOT take her soul. She's going to live. Her death did not happen."

Gee threw her hands up in exasperation. "Yes, we know that. Because YOU stopped it! She was supposed to be crushed in that car. You were to take her soul from her body. Ky was to take her up. BUT, NO! You took her body out and saved it."

My legs gave out as the truth of Gee's words hit me. The little girl from the hospital's words came rushing back to me.

"Don't look so sad. He said this body I have is sick and once I die I will get a new body and a new life. Souls aren't forced to wander the earth. Only those that are too scared to go on are left here to wander. If you chose to leave the earth you will return in a new body and a new life. Your soul will, however, be the same. He told me that the man who wrote my favorite books, The Chronicles of Narnia, said that, 'You are not a body. You have a body. You are a Soul.'"

Dank reached for me before I sank to the ground. I gazed up at him. "I met a little girl in the hospital. She had met you. She was sick and she was going to die and you told her that her body was sick and not to be afraid because she would get a new body."

Dank shook his head with a tormented expression. "I know what you're thinking and no."

I stared over at Gee and she glanced away from me. There was something I didn't know and it was important. I gazed back up at Dank. "What are you not telling me, Dank? Why can't you take my body and let me live life again? I can be with you then once my life isn't appointed to die and you aren't breaking a rule."

Gee shook her head and turned her back to me.

Dank closed his eyes tightly. "You won't come back," he said in a hoarse whisper.

"Why? You told the little girl she would. Gee said I would get another body and I would go on living; that is what souls do." Dank reached out and cupped my face with his hands. His thumb brushed my lips. I hated seeing the pain in his eyes. I wanted to end his pain. Why wouldn't he let me?

"Pagan, the moment I became consumed with you and chose to break the rule everything changed. You're my weakness. I chose you over the rules. Once you are taken you will be kept. I will no longer see you or be given a chance to be near you. I am Death. I can't live with the light and you will live with the light. Forever. Never to return to Earth. I can't resist you so they won't let me keep you." He bent down and kissed my nose gently. I trembled under his touch. Tears burned my eyes. I couldn't stand the thought of never seeing him again.

"And if he refuses to take your body he will be taken as a result. Are you going to tell her that part, Death? Are you going to tell her how you will no longer be free to roam the Earth as Death but you will be condemned to Hell? You'll be as lowly as the fallen angels. If she lives, you essentially die." Gee stood watching Dank with her hands on her hips. "The choice is now. Once your powers are stripped I'll be transporting you down. And I truly hate to go down." She flicked her gaze toward me. "You can live and have eternal life while he burns in Hell with the rest of the fallen angels and sinners, or you can go with me and live in light and let him continue to live the life he has lived since the creation of man. For he is, and has always been, Death."

# Chapter Nineteen

The dark sky began to churn around a core of light. I grabbed Dank's arm with both of my hands as if he was about to disappear. "What's happening?" I asked over the sound of the wind roaring in the distance. Dank shook his head, with his eyes on Gee.

She glanced from him to me. "They're going to take him. Because of you, he will be considered as one of the least. He has fallen. He broke the rules." Gee began to yell over the storm-like winds enclosing the clearing. I let go of Dank and walked forward, knowing I had to stop this and he wasn't going to tell me how.

"What can I do?" I screamed at Gee.

She glanced behind me to Dank. "She isn't like the other humans. It's why you fell for her when no one else ever tempted you. Let her make this choice."

"NO!" Dank yelled from behind me with a fierceness in his voice verging on panic. I ran toward Gee, afraid Dank would stop me.

"Tell me," I demanded. She stared back at me as her glowing features seemed ever more otherworldly. The storm grew stronger. Her blond hair whipped wildly around her creating the appearance of the immortal she was.

"He can only be forgiven if you die. He is Death and he will have to accept your soul. I can only do what it takes to kill your body but in the end, until He is no more, Death has to take your soul."

"NO! I WILL *NOT* TAKE IT! SHE IS A NEW SOUL! MY WEAKNESS WILL NOT CONDEMN HER," Dank roared from behind me as his arms pulled me away from Gee.

She ignored Dank's protest and continued to watch me as the storm grew stronger. I had a power here that Dank wouldn't admit and Gee was too frightened to tell me. She was trying to. The friend I thought I'd made at the mental house may truly be my friend after all. There was no wicked intent in her gaze like I'd seen in the other transporter's eyes. She was pleading with me silently. What was the choice? If Dank refused to take my soul then how could she kill me even if I walked right into her arms? Dank's arms seemed to be fighting against a pull from the storm that wasn't pulling at me or Gee. It was here for him. I glanced up at him and touched his anguished face so full of determination to save me that he was willing to be sucked into Hell.

"I love you," I said, causing his face to contort in pain.

"I'm not a man so I do not have a heart that loves as a human does. I'm an immortal god that dwells with supreme power because I hold the keys to Death. But you are my existence. I am yours." Hot tears streamed down my face as I stared into the face of someone who comprehended an emotion much stronger than my weak, feeble words of love. His arm was ripped away from me by the storm-force wind and he stood like the god he was while a dark funnel formed around him. My heart pounded in my chest and I ran for Gee, knowing somehow there was something I could do. She could take me, I could see it in her eyes. There was a way for me to stop this. Gee watched me as I got closer to her and I noticed the hope flicker in her eyes.

"Help him! Do what you can but don't let them take him, please," I yelled over the roar behind me torn from the chest of Death. Gee nodded and glanced back over my shoulder.

"She made the sacrifice. It's finished," Gee announced with a loud, deep commanding tone. Her eyes came back to me as she touched her hand to my head.

The air around me ceased. No longer could I draw oxygen into my lungs. It took all my willpower not to try and gasp for air. If Dank saw me struggle I knew he would fight whatever force bound him to free me from Gee's power. The cold, damp ground rose up to meet me and I lay limp as the sharp pain of suffocation burned my lungs. The storm around me faded away. I heard no more and felt no more. It was different than before. This time the pain eased away quickly and the darkness consumed me.

The smell of coffee and bacon filled my senses as I inhaled a breath so blissfully sweet it woke me with a start. I sat up and glanced around my bedroom. I was in my bed. I swallowed and my throat constricted in pain. I touched my chest and felt tenderness, as if I'd been punched right over where my lungs rested inside me. It had all been real. Dazed, I stood up and walked over to the window to gaze out into the forest behind my house. Would it show proof of the hurricane-force winds that had swept through last night, fighting to take Dank? The trees stood just as they had when I'd walked into them last night. The leaves blew gently in the breeze. This was wrong. I'd given myself up for Death. Gee could have taken me. I had seen it in her eyes. Had Dank still possessed the power to stop it even with Hell pulling him away? I was alive and I was here in my house, breathing, when I'd asked to leave this body behind and cease my life on earth.

"No," I whispered against the windowpane as tears trickled down my face. "I wanted to die. This existence you have given me is worth nothing with you gone. I can't live with the fact you're no longer..." A sob wracked my body and my legs gave way beneath me as I crumpled to the floor. I curled my body into a ball in an attempt to deal with the pain ripping through my chest. This wasn't an existence I could live with. I'd been so sure that Gee had known a way to save him.

This, this life where Dank was condemned to Hell and I was allowed to continue on as if nothing had happened, would be my own personal Hell.

"Tell me, Peggy Ann, are you always this dramatic?" I jerked at the sound of Gee's voice and lifted my swollen eyes to find her sitting on the edge of my bed. Her long, thin legs were crossed and she was studying me with the tilting of her head. "You're a rather unique human," she said with a smile.

Anger began rising inside me and I stood up and glared at her. She'd lied to me. She had made me think I could stop Dank's fate.

"Woah, Peggy Ann, take the psycho look off your pretty face and breathe deeply." She paused and smirked. "Now that you can breathe, that is." I hated the smirk and the flippancy of her attitude after what had happened to Dank.

"You lied to me," I hissed as I closed the distance between us.

Gee shook her head slowly. "No, I didn't. Honestly, Pagan, stop with the advancing on me thing. It isn't like you can hurt me. Quench the drama, sweetheart. I know you love him. Shit, I figure you have more intense feelings toward him than the measly love you humans so easily give. I mean, most humans wouldn't throw their souls blindly away into an eternity they didn't understand for the sake of saving Death. It was rare indeed."

"You could have tried harder to take me. He was being pulled away by a force stronger than him. You could have killed me! I walked right up to you and offered myself like a sacrifice." I covered my mouth as a sob escaped and the steps of my mother echoed in the hallway. I froze, not sure what to do. My insides felt as if they had been ripped out of me. I didn't have the strength anymore to cover up the pain I was feeling.

The bedroom door opened and Mom peered at my bed and smiled and then closed the door softly. I stood frozen and confused as to what I'd just witnessed. I swung my gaze back to Gee, who was still sitting on the edge of my bed. Mom hadn't been looking at her. Gee turned slightly and patted something with her hand smiling at me. My eyes moved from her to the place I'd vacated after waking up this morning and for the first time, I realized I was still in bed. I took a step closer and peered down at what appeared to be my sleeping body.

"I think an 'I'm sorry' would suffice at the moment. You know, for yelling at me and the awful hissing thing you did. Kinda reminded me of the ones down there and, well, they freak me out." I tore my eyes off my body and stared back at Gee who appeared utterly pleased. "I'm waiting on my apology. Speak, Peggy Ann, you know you can." She puckered her lips and tilted her head from side to side.

"I'm dead?" I asked glancing back at my body. "I mean my body is dead?"

Gee gave a loud sigh. "Yeeeeeees, now let's hear it: 'I am sorry, Gee, for talking to you so ugly when you did what I asked you to.' Come on, you can say it."

I shook my head and studied my body before walking over to the mirror. I looked the same in most ways except all my imperfections where gone. I was a perfect version of me.

"What? Why am I here? Does my mother not realize I'm dead? Where is Dank? Did they let him go? Are you going to transport me? Or am I a wandering soul? Where is Dank?" I felt hope for the first time since I'd woken up. I gazed back into the mirror and touched my face. My cheeks were soft and smooth where tears should have left them wet and tender.

Gee grinned. "It takes some getting use to, the whole being in a body for seventeen years and now you don't have one. You forget and you think things are certain ways and they are not. Like the fact you were sobbing so intensely there on the floor with all your dramatic flair and you knew that your body produced tears so you felt them because you thought they would be there." Gee shrugged and stood up.

"Where are you going? Are you taking me? Where is Dank?" I asked again and she held up her hands as if in defense.

"Okay, first of all, I didn't get my apology and you still think you can start just demanding answers."

"I'm sorry! Now where is Dank?"

Gee frowned. "That didn't sound like you meant it." I closed my eyes and realized that even with them closed I could still see. Weird. "Your eyes aren't closing, Peggy Ann, you just think they are. I explained the way that works already so stop it. You look like you are doing the creepy stare thing souls do.

"Please, I'm sorry. Just tell me where Dank is," I pleaded.

Gee smiled. "Okay, okay fine. The truth is I don't exactly know." She shrugged and walked past me.

"What do you mean?"

She turned back around and smiled at me. "It all is confusing. You let me kill your body but of course lover man wasn't going to take your soul from your body. However, I knew, as did he, that if your soul was truly willing it could leave the body on its own. So, I left the swirling hurricane last night and brought your dead body back here. I knew when your soul came back around from the trauma of killing off your body that it would be the time of reckoning. I waited to see and, sure enough..." she paused and smirked. "Honestly, I never doubted it. I could see your fierceness to save him. I knew it was your soul that was talking and I expected your soul to leave your body. It, of course, did and I should have immediately been able to take you and head on up." She gnawed on her bottom lip and shrugged.

"What?" I asked with relief running through me at the thought that Dank was still Death and he was not burning in Hell.

"Ah, well I'm not real sure. I mean I like you and all but I've got a busy schedule and you have taken up quite a good deal of my time these past few weeks. Well, at least since Dank expelled Ky and I got stuck with the job of making sure Mr. Stubborn released your soul. Anyway, see the thing is I didn't hang around and postpone our departure so I could chat with you and you could ask me a million questions. I, uh, well, your soul isn't coming. It won't leave or there is a force holding it." She sighed and frowned at me.

"I don't know what's going on here. You're a first on all accounts. Maybe Death does have to take your soul after all. I have no idea. My guess is that you had better go get back into that body of yours and live this life. I'm afraid Death hasn't been given a reprieve for his rebellion. If you don't go back to your body then you're going to spend eternity as a wandering soul. I don't have to tell you what a wandering soul is because we both know you already know. You see them all the time. Do you want to have their miserable existence? Look, don't let him have been given eternal damnation for nothing." She walked over to where my body lay, lifeless. "If he has to burn in Hell for all eternity don't let him have to do it knowing you're a lost soul. He'll know. They will make sure he knows. It's all about the pain and torture down there. What a little heat can't do to him the knowledge that you gave up the promised eternity he fought so hard for you to keep is going to cause him pain like you will never comprehend." She stared down at my body. "It's your choice. Get back in and live. Do it for him." Then she was gone.

I stood over my body looking at it as hot tears ran down my face again although now I knew I only felt the memory of tears. I was a soul. I couldn't cry. I touched my face and my body felt cold. The thought of returning to this body and existing while Dank no longer roamed the Earth because of me was unbearable. "You're my reason for my existence, Dank. How can I live without you?" I whispered into the room and knew no matter what pain life would hold for me I couldn't cause him any more pain. I would endure life so he wouldn't have the guilt of my lost soul to torment him. He'd given up everything for me. I could sacrifice an eternity of sorrow, if that's what it took to ease his suffering. I slipped back into bed and felt a warm tingling sensation run through me as I rejoined the body I'd left. My eyes opened and a sob escaped from my lips.

"Pagan, honey? You ever going to get up and come eat?" Mom was standing at my doorway smiling at me, completely unaware that her last visit into my room she'd seen an empty body.

"Yes, um, sorry. I guess being in my bed again caused me to oversleep." She walked over to me and sat down beside me.

"It felt good to have you home last night. You can miss school today if you need a day to get adjusted." I thought of staying home in my room and knew it would be too hard. I needed to get out and talk to people. I needed to see life and find a way to survive it. I wouldn't be the cause of Dank's pain. I'd live, for him.

# Chapter Twenty

Mom had sent Leif on to school without me and explained I would be coming in late. Leif was one thing I had to deal with. If I had to live this existence, I couldn't continue to use him. I would never love him the way he deserved. He was my friend and a source of comfort. Allowing myself to remain his girlfriend not only was wrong for Leif, it was a betrayal because I would never belong to anyone but Dank. I couldn't live that way. Living wasn't going to be easy for me. I needed to cut all the strings that tore at my already damaged soul.

By the time I checked in to school I'd missed English Literature. The halls were filling up with students. I held my books close to my chest and clenched the pink late slip in my hand. I could do this. I chanted the reminder over and over in my head. Miranda came out of the crowd of people, beaming when she saw me.

"PAGAN! Hurray, you came! I've missed you like crazy bad. Now lunch won't be so boring and, Oh my G! Guess what?" I struggled to keep up with her rush of words so it took me a moment to realize she wanted me to react to her "guess what."

"Oh, um, what?" I couldn't even force a smile.

She beamed at me and glanced around to see if anyone was listening to her before looking back at me. "Dank Walker is here. Like, at our school. Like, as in, enrolled at our school. Can you believe it? I mean, I know he went to a high school in Mobile, Alabama up until last year when his band landed a hit song and started playing all over the United States instead of just the Southeast. GAH! Can you believe he is here! At our school? I guess if he had to go back to high school our little quaint coastal town is preferable to somewhere in Alabama. But still, I can't believe this."

I stood frozen as her words registered in my brain. Dank was here? How? The rocker she spoke of no longer existed. Panic laced with disbelief tightened my chest and I had to take a deep breath.

"Where?" I managed to ask, knowing I couldn't mask the desperate expression on my face. Miranda grinned and nodded toward Leif.

"Better get that star struck look off your face. Here comes your man."

I barely glanced at him and reached for her hand. "Tell me

where he is. Please, now." Her eyes grew wide at my sudden breathless demand. She was going to think I was flipping my lid again.

"Uh, um, well around here somewhere," she said in a concerned tone and glanced over at Leif, forcing a smile that didn't meet her worried eyes.

"Did you know Pagan was a big Cold Soul fan?" Leif glanced at me but I didn't have time to deal with him at the moment. I needed to find Dank.

"I have to go. I'll see you later," I said by way of explanation as I headed through the crowd at a run. I fought the urge to call his name aloud.

*"You're going to get put back in that mental place if you don't calm down."* Dank's smooth voice spoke teasingly in my ear and I spun around. He was, of course, not whispering in my ear or anywhere near me.

"Where are you?" I hissed quietly. I heard a chuckle and I jerked to look behind me to see a freshman couple kissing.

*"The picnic table,"* he said simply. I turned back around and headed for the front doors of the school. He was waiting for me at the place I had spotted him for the very first time. I pushed open the door with both hands and took off running.

He was lounging there just as he had been the first day I'd seen him, smiling at me as I came around the corner. I dropped my books and hurled myself into his open arms. A sob wracked my body. He was here! He was here. I couldn't speak so I kept my face buried in his chest, sobbing uncontrollably. I wanted to gaze up at him and kiss him and ask him how, but I couldn't seem to control the well of emotion overwhelming me. He pulled me onto his lap and sat back down on top of the table.

"Glad to see me?" he asked in my ear. His warm breath tickled my ear. I laughed into his chest and nodded, still not sure I could speak. "I would have come sooner but I wasn't sure. I had to wait until..." he trailed off and I pulled back to look up at his face.

"Wait for what?" I asked, needing reassurance that he wasn't leaving. Dank wiped the tears from my wet face with his finger and tilted my chin up so I could gaze directly into his jewel-like eyes.

"I couldn't return until you chose. Apparently, if you made the ultimate sacrifice then my broken rule would be amended." I shook my head, not understanding what sacrifice he was talking about.

"You mean my dying? I did that willingly last night. What took you so long? Gee came to my room and she was as confused as I was."

He smiled at me. "No, not dying, although that sacrifice wasn't taken lightly. However, it could have been interpreted as selfish nature by the Deity. You see, humans give up life when they can't deal with the pain. It's an easy escape for them. The sacrifice I'm speaking of isn't one of dying but of living."

He touched his forehead to mine. "You see, Gee was playing her part. She knew exactly what was happening. She isn't a Deity, but she is an immortal and has been around since the beginning of time. She knew it all revolves around self-sacrifice. A completely selfless act."

I shook my head, frowning. "What do you mean?" He chuckled and I realized it was the most beautiful sound in the world.

"You chose to live a life you no longer wanted just to ease my pain. You didn't want to live without me, yet when you knew it would have made my extinction pointless you couldn't stand the thought. You chose to live for me." I nodded agreeing with him but not sure how this had anything to do with how he was here in front of me.

"My beautiful soul," he murmured and caressed my cheek. "When you gave the ultimate selfless sacrifice, it paid for my wrong. You proved to be worthy of my devotion. Of Death's.....love."

I touched his perfect lips with my fingers, wanting to kiss him. To be as close to him as possible. "So, because I chose life, you continue to exist?" I asked in wonder.

He nodded. "It actually gets even better," he said, kissing my chin and then each cheek, causing me to forget what it was we were talking about. His nearness made me weak with pleasure and a soft moan escaped my throat.

"Ah, that sounds wonderful," he murmured as he ran kisses down my neck and across my collarbone. I clung to his shoulders knowing at any moment I was going to pass out from the pleasure. I felt his warm tongue flick across my skin and I gasped, pressing closer to him, ready to beg for more right there in the schoolyard. He pulled back and his breathing was ragged.

"I get to keep you," he said, staring at me with an intensity that made me shiver.

"Keep me?" I asked, reaching up to kiss his chin and trail kisses down his perfect neck.

"Not here. I can't take much more, Pagan. I'm only so strong," he said in a husky voice as he pulled me against his chest. "You're mine now. While you walk the Earth you belong to me. Nothing can hurt you." I heard a touch of humor in his voice. "It's pretty impossible to hurt what Death protects." I smiled into his chest, wanting to stay in his arms forever. But there were questions I knew I needed to ask. I could bask in his presence later.

"I can stay with you for eternity then?" I asked, watching him. A small frown touched his perfectly-sculpted mouth.

"Not exactly. You're mine as long as you walk the earth. Your body will grow old and old age isn't something we can stop. One day you will have to leave this body and begin a new life."

"I will grow old and have to leave you and then what? Start a new life where I won't know you? Will you wait until I'm old enough and then come see me? No. Dank, NO! I don't want to do that. I want to keep you forever, all the time."

Dank cradled my face and stared into my eyes. "Pagan you're a soul. You must live the eternity souls are given. You don't get a choice. The fact I can love you and protect you while you live on Earth is a gift I hadn't even dared to hope for. This is all we can have. I'm Death; I am a Deity. I am not and I have never been a soul. I take cold souls or souls whose bodies have died and send them to the place they have earned. I was created for this." I shook my head, wrapping my arms around him as if he would disappear at any moment.

"I want to be immortal. I want to be with you always. Isn't there anything you can do?" He shook his head sadly, and then stopped, glancing over my shoulder with an angry scowl.

"Leave, Gee, this isn't your business." His voice dripped the cold ice that only Death could muster. I turned and Gee stood nearby with one hand on her hip, smiling like she had just won a contest.

"Ah, but I don't care. That's the beauty of it," she said brightly and stared at me. "He isn't telling you all there is to know because he thinks your mind is too fragile to understand the complexity. Don't let him off so easy, Peggy Ann."

Dank snarled behind me. "Don't call her that."

Gee grinned and winked at me. "Okay, fine. Pay-Gan"

I glanced back at Dank., "What is she talking about, Dank, tell me. I'll do whatever I have to so I'll never leave you. I don't want to grow old. I want to remain as we are now, forever. I'll go wherever you go. Please."

Dank sighed, slipped his hand around my waist and squeezed. "I'll tell you one day. When it's time. There is a way but, Pagan, it isn't easy. It requires giving more than you could ever know. The choice has never been made and for a soul it would be impossible. Souls are handicapped by their emotions which are much too weak."

Gee cackled from behind me. "Souls are supposed to be weak emotionally but that one isn't weak at all. Give her a little credit. She just made a choice no other soul could or would have had the power to make. Her soul is uncommon or you would have never made it yours."

He gazed at me and smiled gently. "I know." The warmth in his eyes made the rest of the world fade away.

"See ya around, Pay-Gan," Gee called from behind me. I hated looking away from Dank's gaze but I did in order to tell Gee bye. She was already gone.

Dank let out a frustrated sigh. "If you didn't like her so much I would make sure we never saw her again."

I stiffened. "What? No."

He grinned. "Relax, Pagan, she's safe from my wrath. She makes you smile and she cares about you. That makes her forever safe and treasured."

I smiled and ran my hand through his dark curls. "So, Death, what do we do now?"

"For starters you need to go break things off with Leif and I'm going with you."

The idea of breaking Leif's heart was bad enough. The guilt was eating me up inside at the thought of hurting him. I shook my head and gazed pleadingly up at Dank. "Please let me do this alone. You can't be there, it will only make it worse."

Dank's expression remained unyielding. "I'm sorry, Pagan, but I can't let you do this alone. He isn't who you think he is. I don't trust his reaction."

I smiled at Dank's belief that he needed to protect me from Leif. Leif was harmless. He'd be broken but not dangerous.

Dank stood up, placing me on the ground in front of him and slipping his hand in mine. "Pagan, I'm not sure how to tell you this, but... Leif isn't human."

CPSIA information can be obtained at www.ICGtesting.com
Printed in the USA
LVOW132159220712

291114LV00008B/246/P